RORY

A Special Forces Protector Romantic Suspense Novel

NEMESIS INC: ALPHA TEAM
BOOK 4

ANNABELLA STONE

BELLA STONE

NEMESIS INC

#0.5 LINA.

Will their surprise wedding be their downfall, or will it bring them a love that lasts a lifetime?

Navy SEAL Dalton Knight only wanted a night of drinking with his team brothers. The last thing he expected was to meet the other half of his soul.

Lina Maxwell knew she should have stayed at home. Drinking and dancing is so not her jam. When her drink is spiked, a knight in shining Kevlar insists he marries her to protect her from the demons who haunt her nightmares. Will their surprise wedding be their downfall, or will it bring them a love that lasts a lifetime?

#1 DALTON

The war on terror tore them apart. Will a terrorist bring them back together?

FORMER NAVY SEAL, Dalton *Nemesis* Knight thought he had it all. A Navy career he loved. His SEAL Team brothers, and her... his Lina. The war on terror proved him wrong. It cost him everything, including his wife. With his trust broken, he'd had to find a new way forward and a new system he could believe in. Eventually, he picked the shattered pieces of his broken heart up off the floor and built Nemesis Inc. from the ground up. Now he makes the rules, he signs the checks, and his heart is off the table for good. Nobody is ever going to get close enough to destroy him again.

For years, Lina Maxwell has watched him from the shadows. Cheering his successes and mourning his losses. He's always been hers; she's always been his. Neither anger nor distance can change that. The time has come to gather her courage and fix the wrongs of the past. In leaving him, she protected him the only way she could, Lina needs Nemesis to see that she did not betray him, that she still loves him with everything that she is. Her bosses and her mission will not allow her to make contact. Her whole life is an illusion. She no longer has an identity, no longer has a name. As far as anyone, including her husband, is concerned, she never existed at all.

Just when Lina is ready to ignore her orders and step silently out of the dark, a terrorist wages war on Eastern Europe. With Nemesis running headfirst into danger, she will use every contact and source in her network to protect him. Will showing him she's still alive destroy not only their memories but any chance they might have had of a future?

Will this mission be the bandage to fix two broken hearts, or will it finally destroy them both?

#2 CORMACK

His happy sunshine girl didn't deserve to be pulled into his world of fire and brimstone. All he could do was hope like hell he found her in time.

As a Black Ops Contractor for Nemesis Inc. Cormack *Jeep* Ford, has seen the worst humans can inflict on their fellow man—in some of the shittiest hellholes on earth. With a twenty-year military career under his belt, he's not one bit sorry when Nemesis Inc. relocates from Kabul to Montana. Maybe now his boots are firmly on US soil, he can peruse a happy ever after with woman who calls to his soul.

To Willow Black it feels like she's waited a lifetime for her soldier to come home. Who'd have thought a connection made over emails and letters would lead her to the man who makes her heart and body sing. With Cormack moving back to the US full time, she can't wait to see if the connection between them can withstand the test of time spent in the same freaking time zone. Just when she's starting to believe he may be her happy ever after, a terrorist destroys everything she trusts in— dragging her into the terrifying reality of the world's underbelly.

A man forged in fire and brimstone—a woman made for sunshine and roses—and a terrorist determined to make them pay. Can Cormack convince Willow her life's not over? Can she convince him to let her go? Or will their hearts have the final say?

#3 LOGAN

They say opposites attract, but can two such different people really find an everlasting love?

Losing his parents in the south tower of the World Trade Center on 9/11 changed the trajectory of Logan Sensei Winters' life. Once an up-and-coming MMA fighter, the rancher's kid from the Midwest crossed over the line of right and wrong in a haze of grief-fueled fury. A second twist of fate changed his world again. Nemesis Inc. gave him a soft place to land and taught him how to direct the rage living in his soul toward targets who deserve it—tangos and terrorists across the globe became his focus… until fate threw him yet another twist and cast his meticulously organized life into chaos.

Eedana Crawford is tired of the rules. She's over the 'show the world a happy family in their Sunday best' façade her family demands. There is no way on earth she's giving up the freedom she's worked so hard to earn—spending the rest of her days in her art studio, teaching classes and painting pretty pictures—following her dreams. When a request for a commissioned piece turns those dreams into a nightmare, the freedom she loves becomes impossible to keep. But trusting Mr. Tall, Dark, and Deadly who appears when she needs him would be a bad, bad idea. Right?

Eedana is his to protect—even if she doesn't know it or agree with it. But Logan will make sure she survives The Organization's attempt at a power grab. There is no way in hell he's losing another person he cares passionately about. Not on his watch.

She is his to protect. End. Of. Discussion.

Coming Soon in Nemesis Inc:
Rory
Aria

RORY

Nemesis Inc. Alpha Team

They say love is a losing game. But what if the only thing you lose is your heart?

Taking his mandated leave was supposed to be a fun trip for Nemesis Inc.'s Alpha Team, recon expert Rory *Mokaccino* Costa. Leave which lasts all of five minutes when a phone call from a teammate sends him to Paris to rescue Adalyn Cassidy and her son, Sam. Changing things up on the fly and living life at a hundred miles an hour is typically his jam. He'll rescue the divorced author and her kid, send them home, and get back to his vacation. A couple of days in the French capital could be fun… right?

It was supposed to be a first author signing for Adalyn's alter ego, Saffron R. Cassidy. She doesn't do people and isn't overly thrilled about crowds, but she'll figure it out as she goes, and hope she doesn't screw up too much. Passing up the opportunity to be the headline signing author in Paris, a signing which could skyrocket her publishing career, would be a stupid move… right? So how did it all go so wrong?

ANNABELLA STONE & BELLA STONE

She's been beaten, her son is missing, and she has to rely on a complete stranger to save them. A stranger who could have stepped right out of the pages of one of her books. Big, bad, and oh so very swoony, Rory Costa.

He shouldn't touch her.
She shouldn't want him.
Falling in love should not be an option... right?
But what happens when love sneaks in quietly and fills your soul when you least expect it?

ACKNOWLEDGMENTS

NEMESIS INC.

Thank you to my Sailor for always having my back. You have owned my heart for almost three decades, and you will always be my hero—even when you make me insane, and I find pens and crap in the dryer. You and our amazing kiddos, Potterhead and Pottermonkey—you make this crazy life worth it.

Thank you, the family of my heart, who not only claimed me as theirs, (in public I might add…) but who read this story as it was written, answering all my military questions, and helping ensure my information is as factual as possible. Any mistakes I have made are mine. Thank you for the middle of the night conversations and virtual smacks upside the head that were needed to keep me on track.

Thank you to my Operators. All y'all put up with my crazy, without a second thought. You laugh at my silly memes, and you love the stories and characters in my head as much as I do. I am forever grateful to have y'all in my life. #Lovelikeanoperator

I'd also like to take this opportunity to thank the god who discovered that Coffee is an amazing way keeping my eyelids propped open when the characters in my head are yelling out their stories at 3 AM… Without the aid of the coffee gods, these stories would never be written.

#NEVERFORGOTTEN

For the 31 heroes of Extortion 17.

Brothers don't always have the same mother.
Until we meet again to feast in the halls of Valhalla.

Special Warfare Operator
Petty Officer 1st Class
(SEAL/Enlisted Surface Warfare Specialist)
Jon T. Tumilson

PROLOGUE

"Keep your hand on the cart at all times until we get inside the store," Adalyn *Bootsy* Cassidy reminded her son. She was probably way too much like an overprotective momma bear with her only cub for her eight-year-old son, but she couldn't bring herself to care. Sam was hers, he only had her to make sure he was brought up and not dragged up or left to fend for himself as she'd been at his age.

"Yeah." Sam wrapped his fingers around the hard plastic. "I remember."

She dropped her purse into the kiddo seat, wrapped the fingers of one hand through the handle, and pressed the remote to lock Sally, her trusty transit van. The home she and Sam traveled around Europe in.

Thankfully these carts weren't metal, or she'd be getting static shocks all the way around the store. She just didn't have the energy for that today. It made her nuts, but despite all the Google searches and forums she'd scoured, she'd never been able to find a way to prevent it from happening. She glanced left and right before crossing the parking lot to the sidewalk which led to the grocery store.

"Can we get ice cream for dessert?"

"Of course, we can." She ruffled the spikes on the top of his head. Not that they moved, mind you. They were glued in place with so much hair gel; never mind a shower, it would take a chisel to dig it all out. "What flavor were you thinking?"

"Mint chip."

She'd already guessed that might be his answer; when Sam wanted ice cream, his go-to flavor was nearly always mint with chocolate chips. Finding it over here wasn't always possible though. She mentally crossed her fingers; maybe this store would surprise them. "Awesome." She slowed her footsteps as they approached the automatic doors, allowing them to slide open before moving forward. "And if they don't have mint?"

"As long as it's not pistachio, then you can pick," Sam offered graciously. "Every time I see green ice cream, I get all excited and then find it's freaking pistachio."

"I know, buddy, that sucks."

"Can I let go now?" Sam turned toward her, the tips of his fingers barely touching the cart.

"I don't know, can you?"

Her eight-year-old huffed out an annoyed breath and heaved a sigh which would have made her mother proud. "Mom." He hissed the word, his tone telling her she was embarrassing him.

She lived for these moments. Joking with your son should be right up there with Christmas presents in her view. She folded her lips together so he didn't see her grin at the trauma asking him for decent grammar was causing him. She was waiting this one out. This exchange had become a ritual between them at this point. Rather than repeating the question, she paused the cart in front of the fresh produce section and quirked up an eyebrow.

He heaved another sigh and muttered, "May I?"

"Yes." She patted the top of his hair spikes with her palm, refusing to cringe at the crustiness. "Yes, you may let go of the trolley."

"It's a cart."

"Trolley."

"Cart."

"Ha, your yank is showing."

"Not as much as your crazy."

They grinned at each other for a heartbeat before she turned to the shelves to examine the tomatoes. "What do you want for dinner?"

"When do we go to the Airbnb?" Sam leaned down and squinted at a funny shaped cucumber.

"Tomorrow." She'd debated long and hard about spending some of her hard-earned cash on an Airbnb. Only the fact she'd been able to find one next to the convention center here in Paris, where her alter ego Saffron R. Cassidy was due to do a book signing the day after tomorrow, had convinced her to book it. That and the opportunity to soak in a tub for a couple of hours after Sam was in bed. She just had to get through the photos, the hugs, and all the peopling, then she and Sam could go toward the Black Sea in their trusty converted Transit. A couple of weeks exploring the coast and writing as the sun went down was just what her soul needed. Her writing mojo fairy wasn't going to say no to a little sun, sand, and sweet wine either.

"Can we have French toast?"

Hah, she should have known his brain would go in that direction; they were in Paris after all. "When in France…?"

"Yeah." Sam wrinkled his nose at the vegetables. "But with ham and cheese. No rabbit food in them, please."

"French toast sandwiches it is." She put the tomato back

and moved the cart down the aisle toward the fridge. "But we have to at least have some salad on the side with it."

"Deal."

"Grab me one of those prepackaged salad bowls. We can share the healthy stuff." She could compromise. They mostly ate pretty healthy considering they'd been living in Sally for over three years and spent a lot of their time traveling from place to place.

Sam opened the fridge door and peered at the prepackaged salad bowls. He grabbed two off the shelf and held them up for her to see. "Do you want Greek or garden?"

"Has the Greek got Feta?"

"If that's the white salty squares of softish cheese, yeah."

"Then yes, let's have Greek salad. The cheese will make it less rabbit food and more comfort food. Throw that in the cart and we'll grab some eggs. I think we have enough milk in the fridge."

Shopping in an unfamiliar supermarket sucked. You didn't know where anything was and had to walk up and down every aisle looking for freaking eggs. Finally, she found them on a shelf next to UHT milk. Even after all this time in Europe, it blew her mind that milk didn't always go in the refrigerated section, and usually was on a shelf along with eggs, sauces, and many other things.

The sound of glass shattering made her wince.

Please let that NOT be my mini-human breaking something I'll have to pay for.

She spun around to see where Sam was. Instant relief flooded through her when she saw there was nothing near him which was broken, and he was just as confused as she was.

Thank you, sweet baby Jesus.

"Someone's gonna be in trouble," Sam whisper-shouted with his eyes wide. The relief in his voice that he wasn't the one in trouble was clear. God bless her child; he had inherited her clumsiness and if something was broken, one or the other of them was usually at fault.

"Yes, they are." Thankfully on this occasion she wasn't the mom trying to apologize profusely for her child dropping something on the floor and offering to pick it up. She grabbed a carton of eggs off the shelf and put them into the cart. "Let's go check out the bakery and see if we can find some crusty bread for our toast."

"Can we get cornbread?"

"You remember that it's not like at home, right?"

"Yeah." He paused at the squirty cream, peering at the cans. "But I like the one here. It makes good toast."

"Me too." She snagged a can of squirty cream and dropped it in the cart. "Ice cream needs cream, especially if we're going to make milkshakes."

"Really?"

"Yes, why not?" She didn't make the treat very often as trying to keep the ice cream frozen in this heat was a ridiculous affair and getting the mini blender to work on the jack plug to the Transit even more of a drama. But Sam had been a trooper on the drive down from Denmark where they'd been camping near the beach at Sondervig for the last two weeks. He hadn't even complained when they'd gotten turned around on the outskirts of Paris and had been heading toward Germany instead of the city center. "We can make the shakes as soon as we get out to Sally."

"Thanks, Mom."

"You're welcome." It was easy to make her boy happy; squirty cream and the offer of a milkshake. She glanced over her shoulder when voices rose to shouting in rapid French; at least she was assumed it was French, but as she couldn't speak the language unless you counted, 'I'm twelve years old,' which she barely remembered from school, she couldn't be entirely sure. She caught a worried look on Sam's face and reassured him, "It's probably just someone getting excited over the broken glass we heard smash a minute ago."

"Oh, okay. Someone's dad sounds pissy." He lifted one shoulder and took off toward the end of the aisle where they could see the bakery section. He peered into the closed boxes of the display shelves. "They have it, Mom. They have the cornbread."

"Bag it and tag it." She resisted the urge to snicker. Having spent two hours writing a homicide scene last night, the words had just popped out of her mouth without so much as a by your leave.

"Mom." If Sam's eyes rolled any further back in his head, he'd have an awesome view of the inner workings of his brain.

"Sorry. I'll try not to sound like an extra on *CSI* until we're out of the store."

He concentrated on scooping the loaf he wanted out of the display box onto the side shelf and putting it into one of the brown paper bags. Sam carried it down the line of bread boxes and placed it on the scale. He shifted from foot to foot for a couple of seconds before glancing at her over his shoulder. "What code number is it? I forgot to look."

"Fifty-six."

She supervised from a distance as he tapped the bread code into the machine and took the label it spat out. Sam folded down the top of the bag and sealed it with the label sticker and handed her the package to place in the cart. "Do we have ham?"

"We'll get some fresh, as I think the package in the fridge has been there at least a week."

"Ugh, the ham will be alive and moving again."

"Shh." There was no heat in her tone. She knew she wasn't the best at keeping up on dates produce went off and stuff. Sometimes it was all she could do to keep her brain in the here and now and not in the story she was writing. Having Sam made staying in the present a lot easier. There was nothing like a 'Mom, what's for dinner?' to snap her out of a story where heroes saved and got the girl, and back to reality where survival and running were a fact of life. "We'll get some." She turned the cart back in the direction they'd come from. This was why shopping in unknown stores made her crazy. Even after walking up and down the aisles a couple of times, she didn't know where anything was and had to search to find them. As she passed the household items, she tossed in some toilet paper and a lemon scented cleaner.

Clean house and clean butts were extremely necessary when you shared a very small space with a pre-teen boy. Stopping by the refrigerated area, she tossed the prepackaged ham into the cart, then it was off to the freezer aisle to look for ice cream with Sam bouncing along in front of her, peering in the frost covered doors looking for his favorite flavor of ice cream.

When his shoulders slumped, she already knew the outcome before he confirmed it. "There's no mint, again."

"Do you want to pick some vanilla and we can grab some mint essence or some strong mint candy which we can add to it? If we grab some dark chocolate chips and green food coloring, too, we can make our own version."

His face brightened. "Can we?"

"Absolutely." His smile was worth the extra few minutes' effort mixing the ice cream, chocolate, and mint essence or candy would cause. If she had to break out the Google translate, she'd figure out which of the tiny bottles on the shelf behind her in the baking section was mint. If not, then she'd phone her friend Eedana. She had to know someone who could read French. Sam dropped a tub of vanilla in the cart and thankfully she didn't have to resort to calling Eedana as she recognized the mint leaf on one of the labels on the baking shelf, and she added that too.

"Do we have milk?"

"Crap, milk, we forgot the milk." She maneuvered the cart around and headed back to the chilled section. Hadn't she just been thinking about UHT milk on the shelves a couple of minutes ago? "We can't have milkshakes without the milk."

Sam added a carton of milk into the cart. "Are we done?"

"Yes, I think so." She couldn't think of anything else they needed right now. But no doubt the second they got back to Sally, she'd remember something and have to come back inside again. "Let's go check out."

Sam raced ahead, but skidded to a stop when he came to the end of the aisle. "Hurry, Mom, there's no line."

"What kind of sorcery is this, a supermarket with no line to check out?" She glanced over her shoulder, expecting to see a hoard of shoppers with full carts chasing her down to make it to the checkout ahead of her, and frowned in confusion when the aisle was empty behind her, almost as if they had woken up in the post-apocalyptic world she'd written about last year and the two of them were the only human survivors after the disaster.

Wouldn't it be awesome, the stores to ourselves and able to help ourselves to the supermarket shelves?

"Where are all the people?" Sam walked to the next aisle and peered around the corner of the shelves.

"I don't know, bud." A slither of ice dribbled down her spine, but she shook it off. The shopping gods were looking down on them was all.

Nothing to see here.

Nothing to be afraid of here.

But yet she couldn't shake that feeling. The unease swirled in the pit of her belly as she stared at the empty checkout. She glanced from the cart to the door and back again.

Run.

Grab Sam and RUN.

RUN NOW!

If jumping out of one's skin was possible, she would have made it look epic when a man spoke behind her, even if like before, she couldn't understand the words he said. "I'm sorry, I don't speak French." She shifted her cart to one side to allow him to pass, and he went to the checkout and stepped into the space next to the till. "Do you speak English?" One could hope, right? Although she didn't expect the people in the countries they visited to speak her language, sometimes Google translate took what she needed to ask, twisted it up, and spat it out as if there was a heck of a lot of Jose Cuervo involved.

The man cocked his head to one side, studying her for a heartbeat before he nodded. "American?" he asked.

"Yes." She didn't think there was any harm in telling him where they came from, no doubt their accents gave that information away anyway. But the second it was out of her mouth, she regretted doing it. She forced a smile for Sam as he grabbed the bread and put it on the automatic belt.

"I have been to America." The cashier started scanning items. "New York, do you know…"

"New York is a big place."

She narrowed her eyes at her son. It wasn't like him to interrupt adults when they were speaking. Before she could open her mouth and remind him of his manners, the cashier took the carton of eggs and leaned over the counter to drop them at Sam's feet.

What on earth was he doing? Yes, her kid had been rude, but there was no call for this kind of behavior. "Hey, that wasn't called for."

The cashier scowled and pointed a finger at her. "You have to pay for all damages."

Everything inside her screamed at her to leave. This must be the reason there was nobody else in the store. The staff here were unbelievably rude. "You threw them on the floor."

"Actions and words have consequences," the man muttered. "You will pay for them."

He's insane. He has to be. I'm not standing for this crap.

As much as she didn't want to act like the proverbial Karen, there was no way she was going to stand here and let him bully her and Sam. "I want to speak to your manager now." This was ridiculous. "There is no way I am paying for those eggs; you threw them at my son."

"Your son is an asshole."

What the hell is happening?

This had to be some kind of joke, because the French people she'd met previous to this encounter had been lovely. "Get me your manager." She pinned him with what she hoped was a confident stern look. "Now."

The cashier cackled. "Of course, but he is going to insist you pay for the damages."

"I don't care what you think he will do. Get your manager, now." She would worry about being upset with herself for raising her voice later. For now, she was too damn mad to care. She wrapped her arm around Sam's shoulders as he retreated behind her.

"As you wish." The cashier thankfully didn't come past them as he exited the check out and went around the front. "But you aren't going to like what he has to say."

"I'll wait right here." As soon as he was out of sight, she and Sam were leaving. She didn't have the patience to deal with any more assholes this month. One asshole a month was quite enough, thank you. And the lawyer her ex-husband had hired had been hounding her over emails like it was going out of style.

As if the man read her mind, he stepped back into the checkout desk. "I'll just press the call button."

Fuck. Just fuck.

She winced internally at swearing, even if it was in her head. She'd worked hard to curb her potty mouth once Sam was old enough to start repeating every word that came out of her mouth. She nodded stiffly. There wasn't a hope in hell she was allowing this ass—man to know her knees were shaking so hard if they touched, they'd sound like someone knocking on a freaking door.

"What appears to be the problem?" A man dressed in a suit approached from a door somewhere slightly behind her to the left.

Adalyn pulled the cart slightly toward her, putting it between her and this new man. It was more than a little intimidating to face off against two men, with only her eight-year-old son as backup.

Lord, I need a hero like the ones I see and hear in my head. Could you send one right the heck now, please?

But nobody was listening.

"This woman's son threw the eggs on the floor." The cashier leaned over the desk and pointed to the mess on the floor.

"He most certainly did not," Adalyn retorted. "The cashier did that when my son interrupted him." There was no way she was letting this man get away with it. "I agree it was rude of my son to do so, but there is no need for this kind of behavior from your staff."

"I agree, Ma'am."

It was only then it struck her as weird that the manager had spoken in English from the second he'd approached.

"Come with me." He held an arm open in invitation. "We will check the cameras and it will tell us who did what."

"Sir…"

"You stay quiet." The manager pointed a finger at the cashier. "We will discuss the rest when I have looked at the cameras. And get Renee to clean up the mess in the storeroom."

"Yes, Sir."

Shouldn't he be speaking to his employee in French?

"We will just leave." She took Sam's hand and rounded the cart. The only way to the exit was through the row on the customer side of the checkout desk. "I don't have the patience to deal with this right now."

"Ma'am…"

"We are leav—" Before she could finish the words, pain exploded in the back of her head. With the sound of her son's screams echoing in her ears, everything went dark.

CHAPTER ONE

This nightmare sucked. Everything hurt. Her face, her body, even her hair and fingernails. Adalyn shifted, sending bolts of pain through her body and she screamed in her head. At least she thought she did.

"Mademoiselle?"

Who is that?

My dreams are really coming up with crazy daisy things.

Oh my god, I hurt so bad.

Open your eyes and it will stop.

Open. Them. Now.

"Mademoiselle?"

"What?"

"English?" the voice said. "Do you speak English?"

Her eyelids finally did as she wanted and cracked open. Everything was blurry, and the pain didn't disappear. If anything, it ramped up the hammering and drilling inside her head, and the burning flames down her body turned inferno hot.

"Mademoiselle, do you hear me?" A blurry shape leaning over her asked the question.

"Yes, hurts."

Another voice spoke in what appeared to be rapid French and something white was pushed under the shape's chin. He grabbed it with both hands and flipped it open.

Notebook. It's a notebook.

"Yes, you are hurt," the shape said in halting English. "We are the police. We will help you."

Police? This dream sucks.

"The ambulance will be here soon."

Ambulance? What? Why?

She was missing something. She knew it. But her brain refused to work. Every time she searched it, trying to make herself wake up and remember, the hammers in her head increased their tempo.

The voices above her spoke softly and she felt something cover her body. She screamed when it touched one painful spot near her belly.

"It is a blanket," the first voice explained. "You have no clothes."

Naked in a dream, and rather than having some hunky man be the reason, it's a damn nightmare. Figures.

"Can you tell us your name?"

"Bootsy."

There was no harm in telling this dream cop who she was. But she didn't want to. If he wanted her name, he could work for it.

"Boosy?" He mangled her nickname. "This is a name I have not heard before. Is it a family name?"

Was he crazy? What mother with any bit of sense would name her child 'Bootsy'? Nope, this was a name given to her by her best friend, Dana. "No." Good grief, this was a realistic dream, she could even hear sirens and the sounds of a city in the background.

The blurry shapes she could see slowly got less blurry and

she could make out the uniform the man leaning over her wore.

This is all so confusing.

Remember.

You have to remember.

Remember what?

Not what. Who?

Remember.

Searching for her memories hurt like a motherf—but she did it anyway.

Spiky hair and a lopsided smile; finally her mind filled with a picture which made her heart fill with love and her soul ache.

"Sam." The name dropped off her lips on a scream. She pushed through the pain which had pinned her to the ground, bolting into a seating position. "Sam?" She twisted her body, searching into the dark. "Sam, answer me."

"Who is Sam?" The blurriness had retreated, and she matched the first voice to the policeman crouched next to her.

"My son." She twisted away from his hand. "I have to find him." She scrambled onto her knees.

"Mademoiselle, you have no clothes."

"What?" Was he insane? Dream French cop was crazy. Of course, she was wearing clothes. She had a kid; there was no naked sleeping when there was a child in the house. Nope, not a house, van. "Sam!" She screamed for her son. He had to be here.

"Mademoiselle," the cop repeated. He tugged something out from under her. "We can see your bottom."

"What? You are mad."

She heard the rustling of paper. "I'm not angry," he replied after a heartbeat.

She slapped at the hands touching her. It hurt her more

than him as he didn't stop wrapping something around her back as she tried to get to her feet.

"Mademoiselle, you are hurt. Please wait for the ambulance."

"I have to find Sam."

"My colleague is looking for him."

Eedana...

Logan...

They'll help.

Call her.

Now fully awake, reality slammed into her.

"I'm naked?" she screeched loud enough that the policeman winced.

"Yes." He nodded. "Hurt too."

"Phone. I need a phone."

"You need to go to the hospital."

She could see the blue swirling lights flashing at what she was guessing was about a hundred yards away. But she'd never been good at guessing distances. "I need my son. And a phone." She held out her hand, palm up to him. "Please give me a phone."

He sighed heavily.

"You need…"

"I'm not going anywhere until I have a phone and can call my sister." She clutched at the blanket with one hand, keeping it closed as she faced him down. Being embarrassed, hurt, and wanting to curl up into a ball and die didn't matter one little bit. What mattered was Sam. The only people she knew who would help her with no questions asked was Eedana and her man, Logan.

"I'm not meant to…"

"I don't care. Phone, now," she demanded. "Please, I need to call my sister." Eedana was the sister she should have had. That definitely meant she was telling the truth by calling her such. She could see the EMTs coming toward them. "Where am I? A freaking field?"

"Please, Mademoiselle, you are speaking too fast, I do not understand."

"Am I in a field?"

"A park…"

"Give me your phone please, any phone."

"When you get to the hospit—"

"No, now." She lashed out at his chest, which was probably a stupid thing to do, but she didn't care. "I need a phone now."

"Okay. Okay." He reached into his pocket and pulled out a phone. "What is the number?"

"I don't know." Who memorized numbers? Not her. "I usually call her on Facebook."

"Okay." He tapped through the screens. "I don't get the app, but have Google."

"Good enough." She snatched the phone out of his hand. Which she knew was unfair, considering he was only trying to help her, but she couldn't bring herself to care.

Oh, god, I hurt so much.

My back.

My front.

My legs.

My head.

Ouch. Just ouch.

She pressed the screen to tap out the web address and had to bite down on her lip to prevent the cry of pain which raged through her.

"Where did my nail go?"

"This I do not know; they are all gone."

"Fuck. Ow." She didn't need to look to believe the policeman. Every touch she made on the phone screen sent stabbing pain up her fingers, through the back of her hand,

and along her arms. But she tapped in her username anyway.

Shit, what's my password?

I can't remember.

She backspaced on the email and tapped in her author one. Thankfully that password flashed behind her eyes and she tapped it in. She went into the messages box and scrolled down the messages. Most didn't register, but one did. It flashed like a neon sign repeating itself in her head.

Message: Where are you?

She glanced at the name. The organizer of the signing event. Why on earth…?

There was only one reason she could think of that the signing event organizer was asking her where she was. But that didn't make sense. The signing was tomorrow.

"What day is it?"

"Tuesday."

"Tuesday?"

"Yes."

"No, no, no." She scrolled past the message and found Eedana's last message, then tapped the call sign at the top of the box.

"How was the signing?" Eedana spoke over laughter.

Adalyn's voice caught in her throat, and she didn't know how or what to explain. The only words which she would find were, "FUBAR, help me." Fucked Up Beyond All Recognition, help me.

"What?" The laughter disappeared from her friend's voice. "Logan!" Eedana screamed for her man. "Bootsy, where are you? Are you okay? Where is Sam?"

"I…"

"May I?" The policeman held out his hand. He waved the EMTs over. "You agreed you would let the EMTs look at you once you had the phone."

"But."

"I talk, you get put in the ambulance." He clearly hit speaker on the phone as Eedana's panicked voice filled the night. "Bootsy, Adalyn? Jesus, answer me."

"Mademoiselle." The policeman cleared his throat. "Mademoiselle."

"Give me the phone, doll."

Adalyn shrunk away from the two men who approached with medical bags in their hands as Logan Winters' voice spoke over Eedana's. "Dana, text Trev. I want this call tacked, stat." Clearly, he didn't care if who he was talking to knew he was tracking the call. "Who the fuck is this?"

"Monsieur, my name is Officer Aubert, with the police in Paris. We have your… umm…"

"Sister-in-law," Adalyn called loudly. She needed Logan to know how she'd referred to Eedana, and lord she hoped he didn't think she was way overstepping her boundaries.

"Sister-in-law," the policeman repeated. "I do not understand how to speak her name. "Boosy?"

"Bootsy," Logan said. "Is she okay? What happened? Where is her son? Where are you taking her?" His questions came rapid fire. Even she couldn't keep up, although the policeman did try.

"Please slow down," he told Logan. "My English it is not so good."

"Sorry. Is she okay?"

"She is injured; we will take her to hospital. We do not know where her son is. A passerby found her in the park."

"I'm on my way from the United States," Logan replied. He rattled off a number. "Call me on this number and let me know where she is."

"Yes."

"Her boyfriend will be there before me," Logan added.

Boyfriend?

What boyfriend?
This imagining thing is part of being hurt?
It has to be.

"His name is Rory Costa, and I'm telling you now," Logan warned, "he'll be coming in hot and pissed. He finished a mission last night and is still on that side of the world. He'll be there before the end of the day." There was the sound of fingers clicking filtering through the phone. "If their son isn't found by the time he's there," Logan continued, "you do not want NATO and the US Navy involved, because I can guarantee they will be."

"Her boyfriend," the policeman said. "He is military?"

"Yes."

The conversation faded into the background when the two EMTs helped her onto a stretcher and pain engulfed her. "Rory is coming. Rory is coming." Those were words she could hold onto. If she repeated them enough, maybe they would come true and whoever this Rory was would help her find her son. "Rory is my boyfriend." She had to remember the clues Logan had given her. "Rory is coming." Her body couldn't cope with the pain anymore and she passed out as a blood-pressure cuff was wrapped around her arm.

CHAPTER TWO

Rory *Mokaccino* Costa sipped on his beer. Why the hell had he resisted in taking his vacation days for so long? Sun, sea, sand, and all the sexy ladies a man could ever want. He lowered his shades when a woman with a particularly stunning derrière sauntered past him with a sexy swing in her hips. "That's a mighty fine…"

Ring, ring.

He dragged his eyes away from the woman and scowled at the phone screen. "I don't answer calls with blocked numbers." Maybe he should just let that call go to voice mail. Nothing good happened when your phone rang, especially when you worked for Nemesis Inc. Phone calls meant jobs, but those did *not* typically feature a blocked number and he was just getting into vay-cay mode. He tapped the button on the side, shifting the phone into silent mode. The patrons at this exclusive beach would not enjoy listening to his phone yell at him for not picking up. He cradled the phone in his hand, protecting it from the glare of the sun. As soon as it stopped ringing, it started again, this time with number for Nemesis Inc.'s HQ.

"Fuck." This call he couldn't ignore. If the boss or HQ called, he answered, period. He climbed out of the sun lounger and gathered his towel, turning away from the crowds before he hit answer. "Go."

"Mokaccino, why the fuck didn't you pick up?"

He winced. "Sorry, Boss, the call came up with no number. I didn't know it was you."

"Whatever. We have a situation, and you are the closest operator I have on the ground."

That Dalton let it pass without so much as giving him some shit was concerning. "Hit me."

"I need you to get your ass to Paris, stat."

"Boss, Morocco is a hella long way from Texas." Seriously, did Dalton not even think of looking at the map?

"France, dumbass. Paris, France!" Dalton yelled loud enough that a man in beach shorts and flip-flops glanced over his shoulder at him with concern in his eyes.

Rory stilled. Had they found a lead on the fucking asshole King? They'd been chasing him for months. "King?"

"No." He could almost picture Dalton scrubbing his hand down his face in frustration. "A friend of Logan's woman and her kid are in trouble…"

"I'm on my way to the airport." He didn't even hesitate. Logan Winters was his teammate, his brother, and one of his closest friends. If Logan's woman had a friend in trouble, then he would do everything in his power to fix it. "Book me a ticket. I just need to grab my shit from my room."

"Trev has a jet waiting for you, and as luck would have it, a friend of a friend is heading that way too."

"Roger that, Sir." He stuffed the keycard into the slot on the door and pushed it open. "I didn't really need or want to see Agadir anyway."

"Hah, you mean you were striking out with the beach babe—ow—what was that for, Princess?"

"I'm standing right here, fattened up like a cow about to spawn, and you are muttering about beach babes to your buddies?"

Rory grinned at the snark in Lina Knight's voice. Wilting flower and Dalton's wife didn't belong in the same sentence, that's for sure. "He was about to say—"

"Don't try to cover for him, jackass," Lina warned. "I'm pregnant, not incapacitated. I can take you out with my baby finger should I not like what comes out of your mouth next."

Yeah, no, he wasn't going to earn the wrath of the former assassin known as Mamba. He'd never be able to eat or drink anything again for fear she'd poisoned it with snake venom. "Sorry, Ma'am."

"Baby, your team are assholes."

"Yeah, I know, Princess, but they are my assholes, and right now the one on the phone needs to move his ass, stat."

Taking that as his cue to get the fuck out of Dodge, Rory cleared his throat. "Send all the details to my phone. I'll grab my shit from The Four X's and hit the airport."

"Trev is sending it over as we speak." Dalton was back to all business. "Usual protocols, check in at eighteen hundred sharp, daily. Back up ETA approx. twelve hours."

"Copy that, Sir." He hit end on the call and hurried his steps up. He had a plane to catch.

———

"Sir, please fasten your seat belt and prepare for landing." The stewardess paused next to his seat.

"How long to landing?" Rory hit the off button on his laptop and closed the cover.

"About ten minutes."

"Thank you."

Over his time in Black Ops, he was used to being the one

kicking in doors. Going undercover wasn't really something he'd prepared for. But how hard could it be to pretend to be Adalyn Cassidy's boyfriend and her son, Sam's, father? If he got stuck, he could just channel Dalton and how possessive he was with Lina, or how Jeep, Logan, and Rexar were with their women. How hard could it be?

He gave himself a smack on the back of the head and ignored the snort from Gunnar McKinley in the seat across the aisle.

"That's someone who had a stupid thought if ever I've seen one." McKinley snorted. "Dalton has taught you to dish out the head smacks even if he isn't there to do it himself, huh?"

"Fuck you, Gunnar."

"Nah, I don't walk on that side of the street and neither do you." Gunner grinned at him. His face sobered. "Do you want me to come with you to the hospital?"

"No, but thank you," Rory replied. "I appreciate the ride on your fancy ass bird."

"She's comfy, isn't she?" Gunnar agreed. "I'll be in Paris for the rest of the week, so hit me up if you need backup. I can have the boys to your location within the hour." He jerked his thumb over his shoulder to where some of his team members were scattered around the plane.

"I appreciate that." Rory dipped his chin. "The boss will too."

"We owe Dalton." Gunnar lifted one shoulder. "McKinleys pay their debts."

"So does Nemesis."

"Damn straight." Gunnar leaned out of his seat and clasped his arm almost up to the elbow. "Call Dory in Morocco if you need to get a hold of me." He released Rory's hand and sat back just as they landed on the private airstrip.

"Roger that." The seats absorbed the thump of the plane

touching down. "Thanks." Rory unclipped his seat belt and gathered his stuff. By the time the rest of the guys were moving, he was already at the door of the plane, waiting for the stewardess to open it. "Thank you, Ma'am."

"You're very welcome," she replied. "Have a lovely visit to Paris."

He smiled and waved over his shoulder as he clattered down the steps of the plane and across the tarmac to where a row of blacked out SUVs waited. The information from Trev at HQ had told him the first one in line was his.

He paused next to it and frowned. "A Range Rover? Hell, I'm coming up in the world." He crouched next to the tire on the driver's side and slid his hand under the wheel arch, searching for the box Trev had assured him would be there. His fingers closed around it, and he pulled it free. He pulled the key out of the box and hit the locks, settled himself behind the wheel, and adjusted the seats. "I'm coming, Adalyn. I hope you're ready for me to get shit done and get you out of this mess." She'd let him do that, right? She'd better, because agreeing to letting him help was going to be a heck of a lot easier than dealing with a pissed off Logan.

He flashed the lights a couple of times and stuck his hand out the window to wave at The Four X's guys, pointed the nose of the SUV toward the gate, and took off toward Paris. Operation Undercover Love was a go.

CHAPTER THREE

Adalyn jerked awake and bit down on her lip to prevent the cry of pain. It wasn't the bruises, the cuts, or the beating the doctors said she'd taken which hurt the most though. That honor belonged to her heart. Her son was still missing. Nobody would tell her anything. "Enough is enough. I'm going to find him myself."

She braced herself against the pain and shuffled her butt, scooting to the edge of the bed before dropping her legs over the side. Thankfully all the tubes were in one arm, and she didn't have to disconnect the opposite side before she could get off the bed.

"What the f—hel—heck do you think you are doing?"

Her head shot up at the rumbling, growling voice coming from near the doorway. Her eyes widened painfully as she glimpsed his wide shoulders filling the whole door. "What the fuck does it look like, Captain America? I'm going to find my son."

He glanced over his shoulder, stepped into the room, and shut the door behind him. "I'm Rory Costa." He paused when she shrank back. "Eedana and Logan sent me."

"You are my boyfriend."

"Yeah, I guess I am." The corner of his mouth quirked up. "And for that reason, I'm going to ask you again. What the heck do you think you are doing?"

"I'm," she jabbed her thumb into her chest, hitting a particularly painful spot, "going to find Sam."

"I will find him for you." He crossed the room, scooped her up as if she didn't weigh close to two hundred pounds, and placed her back in the center of the bed, leaning over her as he did so.

"Madam Cassidy, what is going on here?"

Both of them turned their heads at the nurse's question. Adalyn glanced over Rory's shoulder at the woman. "I —um—my—"

Rory got smoothly to his feet and turned to face the nurse. "Rory Costa." He offered the nurse his hand. "Is my woman going to be okay?"

His woman?

Caveman, not Captain America on steroids.

Jerk. He's a jerk.

Just as soon as she could figure out a way to lift her knee high enough, it would have an intimate introduction to his private parts. If he thought all those muscles and the sexy charm he was laying on the nurse would work with her, then he had another think coming. She would not stay in this bed when her son was missing.

"Yes." The nurse physically shook herself as if she was trying to combat Rory's charm and reached for the clipboard on the bottom of her bed. She flipped through the pages. "As you can see, the injuries are painful but superficial."

Superficial my ass, there is not a dang thing superficial about them. They hurt like a mother-trucker, but they will not keep me in this bed, damn it.

She listened to the nurse telling Rory how she had no

broken bones, and how lucky she was not to need plastic surgery to prevent scars on her face. They could schedule a meeting with one for the wounds on her torso and stomach. She snorted out loud at that one.

"I need to find my son."

"Baby, we are looking for him." Rory's smoky voice washed over her. She had to steel herself against its alure. He turned to her, cupped the side of her face in his huge, calloused palm, and leaned down to peer into her eyes. "I swear we will find our son. I won't stop until we do."

Oh my GOD, I almost believe that he is Sam's father and my man.

She knew this was make-believe. A ruse to make all the people in this hospital allow Rory into her room. The title of boyfriend went straight into the trash can the second Rory had walked into the room. There wasn't a five-year-old girl on the planet who would call him a boy, never mind a woman. If Sam wasn't missing, she'd be tempted to use him for research. To be able to write how it felt to be wrapped up on those huge arms, or pressed against the wall…

What on earth are you doing?
Sam. Is. Missing. Grow. The. Fuck. Up. Adalyn.
I'm a horrible mother.

"Promise me, you will find him." The words hitched in her throat, but she managed to get them out.

"I swear it." He gathered her gently into his arms and moved her across the bed while climbing in beside her. "I swear we will find him. I have people on the way right now."

"Monsieur."

"You better not have a problem with me comforting my woman, lady." Rory pointed one finger at the nurse. "If you do, then you and me are going to have problems. Big ones."

"Non, Monsieur." The nurse backed away. "I think it is not a problem for now."

"Thank fuck."

"You are laying it on thick," she whispered low enough that she hoped the nurse didn't hear as she left the room, closing the door behind her.

"Nope, I'm not," Rory muttered. "Just doing my job." He tipped up her chin and peered into her eyes again. "We will find him."

"That wasn't what I meant." She pushed against his chest. "Get off me."

"Am I hurting you?" He eased himself back a couple of inches but didn't get off the bed.

"Yes." She lied through her teeth. "How do I know you are who you say you are?" The words had been meant to make him back off, but instead they sent panic racing through her. What had she been thinking? How did she know this man who called himself Rory was the Rory Logan said was coming? Her breath sawed painfully in and out of her chest.

"Shh, it's okay, calm," Rory crooned. He shifted next to her and a phone appeared in front of her nose with the screen open. "Speed dial one takes you to my work."

She reached for the phone, but Rory snatched it back.

"Your hands are hurt."

No shit, sherlock.

"All of me hurts."

Even with the couple of inches between them, she felt his growl as well as heard it. "I'll call." He hit the screen and put the phone to his ear, all the while watching her carefully as moving more than necessary would make her faint from the pain. "Yo, Trev, put me through to Winters' house, will ya?" He nodded. "Thanks." There was a short pause before he spoke again. "Hi, I have someone who needs to hear your voice. Yeah. I'll put her on now."

She carefully took the phone he offered her and put it to her ear.

"Bootsy? Are you there?"

"Dana." She swiped away the tears which filled her eyes with the back of one bandaged hand and shifted the phone in the other. "Please tell me this man is the real one."

"I swear he is." Eedana's soothing southern drawl washed over her, a balm for her ragged, raw nerves. "He is Logan's friend. I've known him for months."

"What does he look like?"

"Captain America on steroids."

The laugh snorted out her nose before she could stop it. This right here was why she and Eedana clicked. Their brains worked the same way. While Eedana made pictures with paint, she herself painted them with words and wove stories to show the beauty of the images she typically saw in her head. "Hmm."

"Hah, you thought the same thing," Eedana whispered. "Is there any word…"

"No." Tears threatened once again but she fought them. They would not fall anymore. Once she had Sam back, then she could cry all she wanted.

"Logan, his boss, and the team are on their way."

That didn't help her right this second. "I need to go look for him." She ignored Rory's snarl. Now that she knew this was the right Rory, she was almost confident that he wouldn't hurt her. If he did, then she would tell Logan when he got here.

"Please wait at the hospital at least until the boys get there," Eedana pleaded. The worry and stress her friend was feeling came through over the phone. "If not for you or Sam, then for me."

"She'll stay here," Rory promised.

"Stop listening." She nudged him with the only part of her which didn't feel like it was being stabbed by twelve thousand needles; her left elbow. "Get off the bed and stop listening."

"Wait!" She winced at Eedana's yell in her ear. "Rory's in bed with you?"

"No."

"Yes."

The asshole was snickering at her. This time she slammed her elbow into his ribs, jolting her body and she had to bite back the resulting pain. "No. He's not." She lied through her teeth. The romantic in Eedana would be swooning and have them walking down the aisle before the end of the week if she didn't put a stop to it. "All I want is to find Sam."

"Let him take care of you," Eedana said. "You can trust him, I promise you can."

Adalyn knew by the tone in Eedana's voice that there was no winning this argument. "Okay."

"You will do as he asks?"

If it involves not looking for Sam, not a chance in hell.

"Yes."

"You are the sister I should have had," Eedana said. "And I'd be an idiot to believe you."

"Agree," Rory whispered softly. "You have a tell, for when you are telling porkies, you know." He pulled her fingers away from the collar of the hospital gown she wore.

She lowered the phone from her ear and glared at him as much as she could with two swollen eyes. "Shut up."

"What?"

"No, no, not you, Dana. The mammoth you sent to help."

"Oh, is he doing the caveman growl?"

"You could call it that," she replied drily.

"Yeah, they all have that down pat," Eedana said softly. "It gets annoying after a while. Lina swears by a skillet someone called Betty told her to use."

"As long as it's for whacking him in the balls, I'm good

with that." Out of the corner of her eye she saw Rory move and adjust his position on the bed.

Cross your legs all you want, jerk, it won't save you if you stop me from leaving here.

"Just promise me that you won't leave the hospital until Logan is there," Eedana asked. "Please."

"I have to find Sally."

"Who the fu—heck is Sally?" Rory straightened in the bed, careful not to touch or hurt her as he did. "Is there someone else missing?"

"Sally is my home."

"I'm confused. You lost your home in Paris? How on earth did you bring your house to Paris?"

He couldn't be that dense, could he? "Umm."

"Wait, do you mean an RV?"

"I'm still here." Eedana snickered. "I just need to laugh so loud I'm putting you on silent for a second so he doesn't hear me baying like a donkey."

"You do not bay like a donkey." But there was no response from Eedana.

"Do you mean an RV? You do, right? It's the only thing which makes sense, unless Sally is a person. And if someone else is missing, then we need to report it."

"Shh. Wait until I'm done." She'd be a fool not to ask him to go look for her home on wheels. He was here, he could do that and while he was gone, she could figure out how to leave here and go find Sam.

His eyebrows flew up as if he wasn't used to someone telling him what to do. Well, maybe he wasn't used to a woman telling him what to do, but she was sure he'd find some brain cells somewhere in that pretty head of his which would help him figure it out… hopefully somewhat fast.

"Okay, I'm back." Eedana hiccupped. "I couldn't."

"I promise I'm okay." She was being stupid and a terrible

friend. "I will be better when we find Sam, but if you are sure who you sent can be trusted, then I'm safe for now too."

Nope, saying the words out loud didn't help with the panic, fear, pain, and rage which competed for top position in her mind.

Rory gestured for the phone, and she nodded in response. "I gotta go, Dana. I love you."

"I love you too, sister. Be safe," Eedana replied. "Put Rory on the phone, okay?"

"Sure. Bye."

"No," Eedana chided her. "Do you not remember from your stories? We don't say goodbye. We say see you later. Goodbye is not for us."

"I remember. I'm sorry." She winced internally from worrying her best friend. "See you later." She handed Rory the phone and laid back against the pillows, listening to his side of the conversation.

"Hey, it's me again."

She could hear the affection in Rory's voice as he spoke to her friend.

"I promise I'll put her on the first plane to you."

What the hell? He was sending her to Montana. "That is not happening." She pressed her hand to her waist when she shot into sitting upright on the bed too fast and pulled a stitch or something. "I am not leaving Paris without my son."

"He might not even be in Paris by now."

"He has to be."

"I gotta go, Eedana. I'll call you later when Logan is here."

The asshole didn't even bother responding to her. Instead, he took his time saying 'see you later' to Eedana. Murder was acceptable under the circumstances, right? Because there was no way just walloping him in the balls was going to be enough. It just wasn't. "I refuse to leave Paris without my son." Her mother always told her she was stubborn as a mule who'd decided it was time to return to the barn. Her momma, if she was watching from wherever souls went after they died, was about to figure out that she'd never seen what stubborn was when it came to her daughter. "It. Is. Not. Happening. Do you understand me?"

"Are you done?"

"Jerk."

"I'm not calling you names." Rory's voice was way too level. "Please don't call me them either."

"If I stop, will you stop trying to send me away without Sam?"

"I don't make that call," Rory said finally. "That's the boss's call, I probably won't get a say." He paused and glanced at her. "You might not either."

She knew a warning when she heard one. "I am not—"

His finger was in front of her lips, not quite touching her as if he knew it would cause her pain. "If you feel better when the boss gets here, I promise to talk to him," he told her, his brown eyes serious. "But the first hint that you are not able and we're done."

As if I'm ever going to show you a wince or an ounce of pain. Thank you for telling me what I have to do.

"Okay."

"Do we have a deal?"

"Yes."

"Somehow, I don't believe you." He huffed out a breath. "But right now we have no other choice. The boys will be here tomorrow." He nodded to a chair next to the bed. "I'm going to be sitting right there in that chair. You get some sleep."

She nodded as she didn't quite know how to respond to him. He nodded and climbed off the bed. She took her time settling herself carefully. If she made a sound of pain, he'd never agree to letting her stay and she didn't know if she was strong enough right now to prevent him from making her leave.

Adalyn's eyes drooped closed, a combination of the medication, pain, and adrenaline dump finally taking its toll on her battered body. "Night."

"Try to rest." Rory reached over and dimmed the light. "I'll be right here. I promise you are safe. To get to you, they have to go through me, and that isn't happening in this lifetime."

She believed him. God help her, she did. She should know better. Hadn't life taught her to never, ever trust a man? Yet here she was, drifting off to sleep knowing this one, this man, would take on the world to make sure she slept in peace.

CHAPTER FOUR

Rory kept his eyes closed, stretched his feet out in front of him, and leaned back into the most uncomfortable chair on the planet. Why did hospital rooms have to have straight backed plastic chairs? A cushion or even a bucket seat would go a long way to making these torture devices more comfortable for families waiting next to their loved ones' beds.

Not that Adalyn was his loved one. But the hospital didn't know that, and he'd be damned if he gave them reason to question his right to be here.

A whimper from the bed opened his eyes, and he turned his gaze to the woman he'd thought would never quit arguing with him. "Shh, Adalyn, I'm still here."

She jerked at the sound of his voice and scooted away from him toward the opposite side of the bed.

Well, that bites.

She's afraid of my voice.

How the fuck was he supposed to help her if she was afraid of him? Maybe he should call the nurse and ask her to give Adalyn something for the pain she must be in. They could add it to the IV she had in the arm closest to him.

"Shh, baby, I got you." He brushed one finger over the back of her hand, and she stunned him into silence when she turned her hand over and grasped it, holding onto it as if it were her only anchor to keep her in the present. If she needed that, he vowed he would stay hunched over the bed for as long as she needed. But maybe she wouldn't mind if he tried to get a little more comfortable. He managed to get the elbow of his other hand on the bed without pulling his finger free, and then his forearm down. He rested his head against his upper arm.

I've slept in more uncomfortable places; it will do.

"SAAAAM!"

Adalyn's scream scared the shit out of him. He'd been listening to her, even as he dozed. But he must have missed something. She went from whimpering in what he'd thought was pain to screaming her son's name. Rory jumped to his feet, searching the room for the threat before he realized what was happening. She was having a nightmare.

The door slammed open and Rory dropped into a fighting stance, his knees bent, one foot slightly behind the other, and his hands raised, ready to block or fight whoever was coming.

"Monsieur, your wife." A nurse stumbled to a stop just inside the door. "We can give her something to help her sleep."

"No," Adalyn cried. "No drugs. I'll be trapped in the nightmares."

"They will stop the nightmares," the nurse promised. She eyed him warily and moved further into the room.

"No, please."

"Enough." Rory knew the nurse only wanted to help. But he wasn't here to make the hospital staff's job easier; he was here for her. For Adalyn. "No drugs. I'll hold her and keep the nightmares back."

"Monsieur, this is not possible…"

"With all due respect, Ma'am, I don't care about your rules. I care about my woman. She's been through hell, and our son is missing. I am getting in that bed and I'm staying there, and there isn't a damn thing you can do about it."

"Monsieur, I will call security."

"Try it," he dared her. "But first, I want her doctor in here." He scrubbed his hand over his head from back to front and back again.

Do not punch her for doing her job.

He stepped between the nurse and the bed. "You are not giving her anything until her doctor is here and you've given us a chance to try it our way. This is not a medical issue. It's a nightmare issue, and ask any veteran on the planet, there is no drug that fixes those." He jabbed his thumb into his own chest. "Ask me how I know."

"How do you know?"

Damn it, he should have known the irony would be lost on a non-English speaker. "Because I've seen more war than any man has a need to. If you want an expert on nightmares, then I assure you I am more than level expert."

The nurse opened and closed her mouth a couple of times as if she couldn't think of the words she wanted to say in English. But thankfully she moved away from the bed before he needed to physically move her. "I'll go find the doctor."

"Thank you." He followed her to the door and shut it behind her. "I'm sorry, Adalyn. I shouldn't have fallen asleep."

"I can hear Sam calling for me." She hiccupped. "He is screaming for me to save him and every time I can just about touch him, he disappears."

He crossed the room and sat sideways on the bed next to her. "I won't touch you unless you want me to." He didn't want to scare her, but if she didn't want the doctor to prescribe drugs the second he got in the room, then she needed to at least look calm on the outside.

She stared at him with those big blue eyes of hers, then scooted across the bed and into his side as if she wanted to burrow into his skin. He swung his legs up onto the bed and wrapped an arm around her.

"The doc needs to think you have calmed down." He scooted himself lower on the bed, careful not to hurt her. "Or I may not be able to stop him from giving you something." He rubbed his chin gently on the top of her head. "At least not without violence, and I think you've seen enough of that for a while."

"Yes. Too much."

"I know." He wrapped his other arm around her, enclosing her against his chest. "Is this okay? I'm not hurting you, am I?"

"Yes, it's okay." She turned her face into his chest. He could feel the dampness on her cheeks from where tears had fallen in her sleep. "I trust you."

Relief flooded through him. It would be impossible to fight the doctors to keep her drug-free if she was afraid of him. This woman, who was willing to let him help. Her he would protect with every inch of his power. He cocked his head to one side and heard the murmuring of voices in the corridor outside the room. "I think the doc is here."

"Okay." The fingers of one hand bunched into the material of his shirt, holding on as if her life depended on it. He knew her life didn't, but right now, her sanity probably did.

He watched the handle of the door. "Three, two, one."

The door pushed open, and a male doctor strode into the room. He scowled at Rory. "Monsieur—"

"Shh, she's sleeping," he whispered as if he was determined not to wake the woman lying in his arms with her eyes closed. "Please do not wake her."

The doctor studied him for a heartbeat, nodded, and went to the end of the bed to pick up her chart. He flipped through the notes, glancing at them multiple times, before he nodded to Rory and left the room again, closing the door behind him.

"He's gone."

CHAPTER FIVE

This was ridiculous. She was better than this. Stronger than this. The too stupid to live woman she refused to write about was not her. Yet here she was, curled up on a hospital bed with her tears soaking the shirt of some hunky alpha male sent to rescue her. "I'm sorry."

"Don't be sorry; nightmares catch the best of us off guard, and you have more reason than most to be haunted by them."

She nodded, her cheek rubbing off his shirt. "I just can't stop hearing him screaming for me."

He heaved a breath which lifted his chest a little more than the previous ones had, as if he was getting frustrated with her. "What can I do to help?"

"Nothing."

"What do you do when Sam is scared or has a nightmare?"

"I curl up in bed with him, sort of like you are now, and tell him a story."

"I'm not much for bedtime stories," he whispered softly. The silence stretched between them, only broken by the sound of their breathing and the hospital machines she was attached to. "What kind of story do you want to hear?"

"What kind of stories do you know?"

"War stories." He snorted. "But I'm guessing those aren't the ones either of us need right now."

"Yeah." Even she could hear the despondency in her voice. "Do you know any fairy tales?"

"Umm, no."

Who didn't know fairy tales? "Not even from when you were a kid?"

"Fairy tales weren't a part of my life that I can remember," he said. "We kids worked on the farm from sunup until it was time to go to school, then again from the second our homework was done until dark." He shifted under her. "Don't get me wrong; my folks weren't mean or nasty or any of that shit. There was a lot of us kids. The farm kept the bank loan at bay by all of us working our asses off every second of every day."

"Same." If anyone understood that, she did. She'd married way too young to try and escape that life. Only to find herself dropped into the twilight zone which she'd never understand. "City life isn't all it's cracked up to be either."

"Is that why you travel so much?"

"Some of it." She forced her fingers to open, releasing his shirt, and flattened her palm on his chest. "After my ex-husband was arrested for manslaughter and my divorce was final, the cold hard truths of living in Manhattan with his family was choking me. I didn't want Sam to grow up around them. I wanted him to know how to treat other people and not to think they were all there to serve him."

"Do you think his family is involved?"

"They don't know where we are. I was careful."

"With enough money to throw at a problem, there are ways of finding out information if you want it badly enough."

"He speaks to his father occasionally."

"That will do it."

"Could they really track us from a prison phone call?"

"Yeah, I know someone who could do that in about five minutes flat."

"You aren't making me feel better."

"Sorry." He brushed one hand over her hair, pushing it back from her face. "I don't know how to sugarcoat shit."

"Please don't lie to me." She didn't need another man, even one who was just here to get her out of this mess and to help her find Sam, who fudged around with the truth. "I'd rather know the truth than sugarcoated shit any day of the week and at least twice on Sundays, okay?"

"You got it."

"Thank you." She could almost hear his brain powering up as he tried to think of what to say next. But what was her excuse? Words were her business; they were how she earned her living. But here she was with absolutely none, at least not ones which didn't sound stupid in her head. "Umm…"

"Yeah, it's weird trying to come up with something to say on the hop, isn't it?"

"Yes." There had to be something they could talk about. At times like this, she wished she was more like Eedana. Her friend might think she was shy and reserved, but that was an illusion. The second Dana knew someone, she was a chatterbox who didn't care if she stumbled over her words or mixed stuff up.

Eedana…

I'm a genius.

"Tell me about Eedana." She lifted her head off his chest to look at his face. "About how she's getting on at the ranch."

"You want me to…" Both his eyebrows flew into his hairline, and he waggled them at her. "…Gossip?"

"Yes. Please."

"Umm. Men don't gossip."

"You do now, Mister."

"Am…"

"Three, two, one, gossip."

"I'm more used to, three, two, one, engage or fire."

"Not this time, you're stalling."

What are you doing?

Why the fuck are you flirting when Sam is out there missing?

Stop it.

"It's okay, you don't have to. It was a stupid idea."

"I'm thinking," he said. "Gimme a sec."

"You don't—"

"Lemme me think a second, woman."

"Don't call me woman in that tone of voice."

"I'm not using a tone of voice," he replied. "This is just how I speak."

"Whatever."

"Oh, look at us." He snorted. "Is this our first argument?"

"We aren't arguing," she muttered. "We're bickering."

"Same thing."

"Nu-uh." She shook her head. "Bickering isn't arguing."

"Your friend Eedana wouldn't agree," he told her. "There was this one time… did she tell you about Bison?"

"Her pony?"

"Miniature horse, but yeah, him." His hand stroked up and down her back, but she didn't think he was aware he was doing it. "Logan's big stallion fell in love with Bison and got himself stuck in the barn. They had to cut open the side wall to get him out."

"Why didn't they just turn him around?"

"Because that horse is a killer for everyone but Logan and Dana. There is no way in hell Logan is getting in striking distance of his rear hooves. And even less chance of him allowing Eedana be the one in danger."

"He loves her."

"Logan? Yeah, he does. I never thought Winters would fall. Seeing him land flat on his face and scrambling to get her to believe he loved her and what they shared was the real deal was epic." He smiled against her head. "I needed a lot of pops for that one."

"Pops?"

"Popcorn."

"I have an image in my head of a bunch of Black Ops operators lining up chairs like they were at the movies with boxes of popcorn to watch the show."

"Pretty much." He paused. "You know what we do, huh?"

"Am I not supposed to?" She was guessing the answer to that was no. "I kinda guessed and Eedana didn't deny it." There was no way she was getting her friend in trouble, so she tagged on, "Logan either," at the end.

"The boss was not thrilled."

"Is he as scary as Eedana thinks?"

"Dana thinks Nemesis is scary?"

"I thought his name was Dalton."

"It is, but at work, he's more known as Nemesis."

"What are you known as?"

"Mokaccino."

She had to have misheard that. "Mokaccino?"

"Yeah, my last name is Costa—"

"Like the coffee shop?"

"Yup." He lifted his hand off her back to scratch his nose. "When we give names, they are either really obvious and come from our names, or they are part of an inside joke."

"I'm guessing Nemesis didn't get his nickname from his actual name?"

"Hell no, the Taliban called him the Nemesis of Ramadi," Rory explained. "One of the interpreters told Jeep and it stuck. If only they knew how big a heart that man has, especially when it comes to the people he loves."

"Jeep?"

"Our second in command, Cormack Ford."

"Ford to Jeep, makes sense to me. You couldn't exactly go calling him T-Rex or Dinosaur with a name like Ford."

Rory laughed so hard he shook the bed and her sore spots ached and stung. "We have a T-Rex too."

"So, he did a Jurassic Park and was brought back to life from extinction?" She didn't even bother to stop the giggle which hurt everything when it escaped her lips.

"Kinda; we thought he was dead for four years, but he was a POW." The side of Rory's mouth quirked up in a smirk. "But he had that nickname for years before."

"Why?"

"Why T-Rex?"

She nodded. She needed to know the answer.

"His first name is Rexar."

"Ah, that makes more sense." She nodded. "But I've never heard the name Rexar before."

"His family is from the south. It's a family name, I think. His twin is Draxer. At least, I think that's his full name. I just know him as Drax. Two of the hardest bastards I've ever had the pleasure to fight beside, even if Drax is a different branch to ours."

"I'm guessing one of you is Army and the other Navy."

"Yeah."

"You're Army," she guessed.

He huffed and reached for the water glass on the table next to the bed. "Wash your mouth out. I don't have soap yet, but I'll get it for you if you keep saying that," he teased lightly.

"Ah, a frogman."

He pressed the glass into her hand. "And proud of it."

"I can hear it." She took a sip of the water and handed him back the glass, and he replaced it on the table. "What's Logan's name?"

"Sensei."

"Because he's so zen?"

"Heck no." Rory snorted. "Because he's kickass at martial arts."

"You mean 'wax on, wax off.'" She tried her best to imitate the voice from *The Karate Kid*.

"Yeah, like Mr. Miyagi."

"Awesome. Sam and I love that movie."

"You'll watch it with him again," he promised. As if sensing her mood dropping, he quickly changed the subject. "We have two more on Alpha Team. Do you want to know their names?"

"Yes. Please."

"We have Devil Man…"

"Lemme guess, his name is Lucifer." She was only half joking. But when his face turned serious, her eyes widened. "Really? His name is Lucifer?"

"Yup, he works mostly out of Europe these days, but is on a job with his partner Roman's team."

"Ah, that's why you drew the short straw and had to come save my butt."

"And a pretty butt it is." Rory squeezed his eyes shut as if he hadn't meant to say that. "Not that I've seen it given how you are lying on it and all." He slapped his hand off his forehead. "I'm an idiot; please forget I said that."

It was her turn to change the subject and let him off the hook. "Don't worry." She petted his belly. "Who's the last man?"

"Hm, woman; that would be Snow."

An image popped into her head. "Because she looks like Snow White?"

"Not quite," Rory muttered. "Because her hair is white as… snow."

"Snow." She lifted her hand and tapped his. "Jinx." She laughed softly at the confusion on his face. "Have you never done that when you say the exact same word at the same time as the person you are talking to?"

"No. Is that a thing?"

"Kinda."

"Okay."

"Sam will school you on it when we find him."

"Keep thinking that way and I promise everything will be okay."

"Mokaccino, what the fuck?"

CHAPTER SIX

Only the need to keep from hurting Adalyn kept him in place when Logan's voice filled the room. He'd been so engrossed in her that he hadn't even noticed the door opening, or Dalton and Logan entering the room.

Shit.

"Hey, Sensei." He stroked his hand up and down Adalyn's back, trying to keep her from freaking out at the amount of testosterone which just walked in the door. "Hey, Boss."

"What the fuck are you doing?" Dalton glanced at Adalyn. "Sorry, Ma'am."

"You are scaring her."

"No, he's not scaring me," Adalyn muttered. "But he is pissing me off and that makes me want to whack him upside the head with something hard."

"My wife says the same thing." Dalton approached the bed. "I'm Dalton Knight. This is Logan Winters, your friend Eedana's man."

"Hi."

"Hey. Dana sends her love." Logan scowled at him when

Rory smirked at him delivering his woman's message like a good boy. "I'll make sure you get to her in one piece."

Rory felt her stiffen against him and knew what she was going to say before she opened her mouth.

"I'm not leaving Paris without my son." She glared at Dalton and Logan who were exchanging glances. "I will not let you bully me into it either."

"I call the shots here," Dalton reminded her. "Mokaccino, get your ass out of that bed. I want to talk to you outside a minute."

"No." He kept his tone firm but neutral. He didn't want to piss off his boss, but he'd promised her he'd help her. Leaving her wasn't that, in his book.

"Excuse me?" Dalton's voice went so low and cold he could feel the ice dripping off every word. Typically, that tone would have his boots moving and his ass in gear before Dalton had finished speaking. This time there wasn't a chance in hell of that happening.

"Sorry, Boss, I gave Adalyn my word."

"It's okay, Rory," Adalyn whispered. "They aren't going to whisk me out of the room and ship me back to the US when your back is turned."

Don't bet on it.

"Not until you give me your word that won't happen, Boss." He could be as stubborn as the rest of them. Sure, he didn't show that side of him very often. But Nemesis Alpha Team was about to figure out the lessons he'd learned by being a farm kid with a bunch of siblings. He'd known the art of warfare and having eyes in the back of his head with the best of them. If he hadn't had such good situational awareness, his ten-year-old self would have been hanging upside down by the ankles off the oak tree on the back of their property, missing dinner while his brothers and sisters insisted they hadn't seen him all day.

"Seriously?" Dalton scowled at him. Rory knew there would probably be repercussions for his insubordination, but he couldn't find it within himself to give one single flying fuck about it.

"Yes, Sir." He nodded. "If you give me your word that she stays here until we are back, and she isn't sent anywhere without her agreement…"

"Fine."

Yeah, no, he'd known Dalton long enough to know his boss was level expert when it came to loopholes. "Say it in plain words."

"You have my word."

"Nemesis." He barked out the name. "I'm not speaking to a five-year-old trying to make sure there is a loophole to get pie later. What are you giving me your word on?"

"You are skating very close to the line," Dalton warned.

Yup, don't I know it? It's lit up like a damn rainbow in my head.

"Sir…"

"Mr. Knight, are you always this obtuse?" Adalyn asked. "Because I can tell you seem in kinda a hurry. If you give Rory what he wants, this may all just move along a little quicker."

"No, I'm not." Dalton scowled at Rory and Logan when they both snorted. "You are telling me you and my man are a team now. Is that it?"

"Yes, that's what she's saying."

"Sort of."

He smiled down at Adalyn when she answered at the same time he did. "Is this one of those jinx things?"

"No." She shook her head, her hair brushing against his chin. "Different words, even if they were at the same time."

"Winters, what the fuck are they talking about?" A clearly exasperated Dalton turned to Logan for answers.

"Sir, I don't know." Logan dug into the pocket in the front of his camo pants. "But I can call Dana and ask her."

"Jesus, do not call your woman for answers."

Rory hid his snort of laughter in Adalyn's hair. He was already walking a very fine line with Dalton, but knew he failed when Dalton planted both his hands on his hips and glared at him.

"Okay, I give you my word she will still be in this room when we are done talking."

"Thank you, Sir." Rory dipped his head to whisper to Adalyn. "Will you be okay here?"

"Yes," she whispered back, then raised her voice so Dalton could hear her. "He doesn't look like a man who wants to piss off his wife, and I'll call Eedana if he breaks his word."

"I never break my word," Dalton grumbled. "Ever. My Lina would never believe I did."

"Do you trust him?" Adalyn asked.

"Yes." He didn't hesitate. "Me and Dalton may butt horns every now and again, but if he gives his word, it's a done deal."

"That's good enough for me. I'll be okay, while you—er —talk."

That one sentence told him that she knew there would be answers required for why he gave her his word. "Will you be okay here with Logan?"

"Yes. Eedana would withhold sex for at least a month, if not two, if he was an ass to me."

"Hah, I knew I liked your friend." Dalton finally dropped his stern façade and grinned at Adalyn. "Come on, jackass," he ordered Rory. "Let's get this over with."

Adalyn nudged him with her elbow. "I promise I'll be fine."

He didn't know why he was hesitating; he just knew he was, and he needed to get over it, really freaking fast. "Okay."

He pressed a kiss to the top of her head and climbed carefully off the bed. "I'll be back in a few minutes," he promised.

"I'll be here."

He nodded to Logan and followed Dalton out the door of the room. Just like he'd suspected, Jeep and Snow flanked either side of the door, making sure nobody entered.

"What the fuck was that all about?" Dalton bunched his fingers into the collar of his shirt and slammed him against the opposite wall of the corridor. "I sent you here to look after her, not jump in her damn bed and make all kinds of promises you are not authorized to make."

"Boss, she had nightmares." He wasn't trying to justify it, but he wanted to make damn sure Dalton understood. "Her kid is missing. She can hear him screaming in her head."

"Fucking hell." Dalton pushed his arm into Rory's chest once more and released him. "Does she remember anything?"

"I didn't ask her," he admitted. "She's not exactly calm, and I didn't want to upset her more when I didn't have backup. She did mention an ex-husband who's in jail doing time for manslaughter. It's possible they are involved, but until Trev looks into it, we can't be sure."

"Okay, I'll call him in a few minutes," Dalton said.

"You mean you were afraid of a few tears," Jeep muttered behind them.

"Fuck you, Jeep." His hands clenched into fists, and he had to work harder than he'd like to keep himself from hitting his 2IC. He managed to keep his hands to himself, but barely. "If your wife cried, you'd be on your knees."

"Exactly." Jeep drawled out the word. "My. Wife." He nodded toward the room door. "She is not your wife, Rory, no matter what cover story we gave you."

"Fuck me." Dalton scrubbed his hand down his face. "Have you lost your damn mind and fallen in love with her?"

"What? No," he reassured him. It wasn't love; it couldn't

be. He'd just met her. "If she was one of my sisters, I'd want someone like me to have her back."

"Sure, sure," Dalton sneered. "You keep telling yourself that." He turned on his heel and marched off toward the elevator. "Come with me."

"I'm not leaving this hospital without her."

"Keep your pants on, lover-boy, I'm not asking you to," Dalton replied. "We need to go talk to her doctor, and I have someone to visit for my wife. You are coming with me as backup."

Backup in a hospital? Has he lost his damn mind?

"Yes, Sir." He followed Dalton to the nurses' station around the corner from the elevator. As the staff here knew him as Adalyn's boyfriend, partner, or husband, he wasn't entirely sure which conclusion they'd drawn based on the information they'd been provided. He stepped up to the desk. "I'd like to speak to the doctor in charge of Adalyn's treatment, please."

"One moment, Monsieur Cassidy, I will page him for you."

Cassidy, they clearly think I'm her husband. I can work with that.

"Thank you." He and Dalton moved to one side to make room for a woman who approached the desk as the nurse called for Adalyn's doctor over the PA system.

"The doctor will be with you shortly," the nurse called to them, then turned away to deal with the other woman.

Rory didn't want to get back into the discussion on Adalyn and decided to head Dalton off at the pass. A comment Dalton had made earlier gave him the perfect opportunity. "Who did you want to see that's here?"

"Do you remember Lina spoke about the elderly lady, Caroline, who helped her out a few times?"

"Yes, she lives in Paris, doesn't she?"

"Yup." Dalton stepped back to make room for a nurse pushing a wheelchair. "Lina called her to ask if we could stop by. She wanted me to give her some groceries and shit."

"Ah." He started to put the dots together. "She's in here too?"

"Yes, broke her hip about three weeks ago." Dalton winced. "Lina wanted to come herself, but there is no way I'm letting my wife who's been pregnant for about as long as an elephant to fly trans-Atlantic. I promised I'd visit Caroline and make sure she has everything she needs."

"That's nice of you." He peered around the corner, checking Jeep and Snow still guarded Adalyn's door.

"I keep telling you all that I can do nice." Dalton smirked. "I just don't feel like doing it very often."

"Or unless your wife tells you to do it."

"True."

"Monsieur Cassidy?"

It took him a hot second to realize the male voice was calling him and not some other patient with an English sounding name.

"That's us." Dalton nudged him with his elbow.

"Yes, that's me," Rory obediently answered the doctor he recognized as the man who'd come into the room last night while Adalyn had pretended to sleep in his arms. "I wanted to ask when my wife will be well enough to leave." He gave himself a mental pat on the back for remembering the hospital appeared to think they were married even though the police thought they were a non-married couple. Hopefully they'd be out of here before *that* became an issue.

"Ideally, we would like to keep her for another couple of days." The doctor's voice was tinged with a slight British accent as if he had studied or worked there for a time.

"Would moving her cause any medical issues?" Dalton asked.

"Why would you want to move her?"

"You are an emergency trauma hospital," Dalton said. "It is a matter of safety—"

"I'm sorry," the doctor interrupted Dalton, as if he'd just realized it wasn't Rory he was talking to, "who are you, and why should I listen to you?"

"I'm sorry, Doctor," Rory said. "This is my commanding officer. In the jobs we do, we have gained a lot of enemies. Our concern is that my wife and son were targeted by them. If they know she's alive, they may come here and try to rectify that."

"It's not ideal," Dalton added. "We understand the need for medical care. We do have a medic with us though."

"You do, huh?" The doctor appeared to be considering what they said. He went behind the desk and nudged the nurse out of the way. "Let me look at her results before we decide."

"Okay." They stepped up to the desk and waited for him to read through the information.

The doctor pulled his glasses off his face and pinched his fingers into his eyes. "Okay, most of her wounds, while painful, are superficial," he said. "After I've talked to your medic, I'll make the decision. That's the best I can do."

"I'll take it," Rory said. "Thank you."

"Call Snow," Dalton ordered, then turned back to the doctor. "Our medic will be here in about two minutes."

The doctor glanced at his watch as Rory turned away. He didn't hear what he said to Dalton as he was already at the corner of the corridor, and he put two fingers in his mouth and gave a sharp whistle.

Both Snow and Jeep turned their heads toward him. Rory held up four fingers and made a come here sign, silently telling Snow she was needed.

Snow glanced at Jeep who nodded, and she walked toward Rory. "What's going on?"

"The doc wants to talk to our medic before he'll release Adalyn."

"Jeez, you slap some butterfly stitches on someone one time. One." She held up one finger. "And suddenly you've earned the title of medic."

"Shh, he'll hear you."

"You didn't even notice that I said it in Farsi." Snow poked at him. "Get your head in the game, Mokaccino."

Shit, she's right. I did miss that.

"Hello." Snow offered her hand to the doctor. "I'm the medic." Cautious as ever, she didn't give her name and would wait for Dalton to give her a clue on if she was to use her call sign or her real name.

"Snow, this is Doctor…" Dalton scanned the man's chest. "Doctor Baillairgé. Doctor Baillairgé, our team medic, Snow." Clearly, their boss had decided the good doctor having Rory's fake name and Dalton's real name was enough for now, and everyone else would be referred to by their call signs.

"Nice to meet you." The doctor shook Snow's hand. "Tell me your credentials."

"Iraq, Afghanistan, Africa, South America." Snow lifted one shoulder. "The official places are classified and will have to come from my boss." She nodded toward Dalton, and shrugged again, as if she was sorry she couldn't tell him more. "But if you are asking if I know how to care, clean, stitch, and look after wounds, then I can tell you the US government thought I could for almost ten years."

Rory internally snorted. Aria Keane was one hell of a sniper, and most of her time was spent on rooftops or in a sniper's nest as she protected them with her scope and weapon. She was more apt at causing the wounds than she was at fixing them. But there was no way in hell he was going to bring that nugget of intel to the good doctor's attention.

"Okay." The doctor sounded dubious, but clearly the implications of having the wife of an operator on his wards when she could leave without endangering herself was starting to sink in. "I want to go over her notes with you before I sign the paperwork."

"That's good for me," Snow replied.

Rory knew for a fact the cheerfulness in her voice was faker than a Prada handbag on the streets of New York. But he also wasn't going to call attention to that fact either.

"Rory, you're with me." Dalton nodded to the doctor. "You fill Snow in. I have to run an errand for my wife."

Damn it, he wanted to know the full extent of Adalyn's wounds so he knew exactly what he needed to do to the bastards who'd caused them. But he decided he'd pushed Dalton far enough for one day and followed him to the elevator. "Yes, Sir."

CHAPTER SEVEN

Oh, boy, if she'd been on her own, she'd have cheerfully fanned her face. Eedana sure knew how to pick them.

"Can I get you something?"

"I'm okay." Adalyn tried not to wince as she straightened against the pillows. They'd been making small talk for almost two hours, and she was running out of things to say. While it was awesome to get to know the man Eedana loved, it was awkward as hell for her to do it without her friend here as a buffer. "Hospitals aren't exactly built to be comfortable."

"I know, right?" Logan pulled his phone out of his pocket. "Do you want to see some pictures of Dana and the ranch?"

"Can I?"

"Sure." Logan thumbed through the screens. "I'm not much for taking pictures, so there isn't a lot."

"What about your Facebook or Instagram accounts? Do they have more?"

"Ah... no social media." He grinned at her sheepishly. "I don't mind Dana having hers, but I don't have one." He handed her his phone. "Just scroll through until you get to the end."

"Thank you." She peered down at a beautiful view which took her breath away. "The ranch is in the Crazy Mountains, right?"

"Close enough." Logan leaned over to look at the photo. "That's them in the distance."

"It's beautiful." She swiped to the next picture and didn't even care that the cut in the corner of her lip split again when she smiled wide at the happiness on her friend's face. "Never hurt her." The words she'd been threatening Dana with for weeks popped out of her mouth. "If you do, I'm telling you now, I will find you and make you pay for it."

"Or you'll put me in a book, Miss Author Saffron R. Cassidy, and kill me off, is that it?"

"That too."

"I can see why my girl loves you."

"Don't think I don't see you turning on the charm, mister." She swiped to the next picture. "You are engaged to my friend, remember?"

"I am, aren't I?"

When he smiled, his whole face transformed from blank to filled with love. There had to be a trick to how these people did that. She needed to remember to ask Rory about it so she could use it for a plot line at some point.

They both turned toward the door when it opened. The doctor she remembered from yesterday and a woman with hair so blonde it was almost white walked into the room, followed by a nurse. The blonde woman had to be Snow, the teammate Rory had told her about.

Man, I'd kill for hair like hers.

"Snow?" Logan rose from the chair next to her bed.

"We're springing Adalyn." Snow grinned at Logan. "Tell Eedana she'll be home soon."

"I'm not leaving until we find Sam." It didn't matter how

many times she had to keep repeating herself. It was not happening.

"I'm talking about leaving the hospital," Snow said. "Rory might shoot us if we said you have to be out of his sight before we find your boy."

At that moment, Rory and Dalton came back. Rory scanned the room and lasered in on her. "What happened?"

Of course, he noticed she was upset. Or maybe it was the mad he recognized. She couldn't be sure which showed on her face, probably both. "I'm not leaving this country without Sam." These people better get used to listening to a broken record. She would keep repeating herself until they believed her.

"Beautiful." Rory nudged Snow out of the way and leaned in close to Adalyn. "I swear we are not leaving without him. We will find him." He cupped her cheek with his palm. "I swear we will find him."

"I know." She allowed him to tug her into his chest. Even if it was all for show for the hospital staff, she couldn't bring herself to resist the comfort he offered. Fake or not, comfort was comfort and she'd more than earned it.

"Excuse me." The nurse cleared her throat. "I need to take out the IV and disconnect everything."

"Of course." Rory pressed a kiss to the top of Adalyn's head before he stepped back to let the nurse approach.

The IV pinched on the way out and she winced. Rory growled and she lifted her gaze from her arm to his face. "I'm okay, Moka, I swear." Out of the corner of her eye she saw Logan splutter around the water he'd just sipped when she shortened Rory's nickname. "What? You act like you've never called him a brand of coffee before," she said as Dalton thumped Logan on the back.

"Not." Logan stepped forward at the force of a particularly vigorous blow to the back from Dalton. "We've never called him Moka."

"I am not calling him what you all do." It was official; her snark had remembered she existed and was making its presence known. "I get to call him the name I chose, and you all get to not tease him about it."

"Fuck," Rory whispered softly.

"What?" She'd completely forgotten the nurse was still detaching her from machines and had stopped when her arm didn't move as far as she'd thought it would when she turned toward him.

"Now they'll call me it for sure."

"Then that's what baseball bats are for." She pointed to his knees. "They are awesome for reminding men who's boss."

"Bloodthirsty, my Beautiful." He grinned at her. "Y'all heard that, right? If you mention it, my *wife* gets to kneecap you with a baseball bat."

"You all are crazy." The doctor pushed a clipboard in front of her. "You need to sign here." He flipped over the first page and pointed to a spot at the end of the second page. "And here. This absolves the hospital of any responsibility should you have a relapse of any kind."

"Okay." She took the pen he offered and scribbled her name across both spots. She didn't care if they were asking her for every dollar of royalties her books earned over the next fifty years. If it got her out of the hospital and closer to searching for Sam, then she'd give it.

"Thank you." The doctor took the clipboard back. "Good luck to you all." He pinned Adalyn with a look. "Listen to your medic and your body. Stop when either tells you that you've done enough."

"Sure."

He huffed out an annoyed breath. "I'm sure that is similar

to when my wife says fine." He nodded to them all and left the room, clearly not needing a response to his question.

She was so ready to get out of here. But as she swung her legs out of bed, she realized she was naked under the hospital gown. "Umm."

"What is it, Beautiful?" Rory was right next to her.

"I don't have any clothes."

"Shit." He spun around as the nurse reached the door. "Nurse, does this hospital have a gift shop which sells clothes?"

"No, I'm sorry." She shook her head. "But there is a department shop down the street which should have what your wife needs."

"Thank you."

"You're welcome." The nurse smiled at them. "I hope you feel better soon, Mrs. Cassidy."

"I'll go," Snow offered. "At least I won't buy her camo and all black clothes."

"Here." Rory dug into his pocket and pulled out a handful of cash. "Buy anything you think she'll need for at least a few days until we can get her vehicle."

"Sure thing." Snow put her hand on the door and called over her shoulder, "Move your ass, Sensei, you're with me."

Adalyn covered her face with her hands. She didn't remember the last time she'd had to rely on someone else to pay her way. Maybe when her ex-husband had been sent to jail.

"Hey?" Rory gently pulled her hands away from her face. He crouched in front of her. "What's wrong?"

"I'll pay you back."

"Stop it; we all need a little help sometimes. Don't worry about it. I don't have anyone else to spend my money on. Let me spend it on you for now, okay?"

"Thank you." Even if he was incredibly kind about it, she was still mortified. "I appreciate it."

"I hate to break up the mushy shit," Dalton said. "But if you are staying, then we need to set some ground rules."

Ah, there he was; the ball breaker. But she was grateful enough that he was changing the subject that she reined in her snark and nodded. "Go on."

"Mokaccino, you are on personal bodyguard duty," Dalton said. "Anything which happens to her comes out of your ass."

"I don't need a babysitter."

"Yes, Sir." Rory patted her shoulder gently. "And yes, you do. Until we find Sam and figure out who did this to you, then we don't know if you are still in danger or not."

"Listen to him," Dalton advised. "For once in his life, he's actually making sense." He glanced at his watch. "I'm going to call my wife and tell her that we're staying at Caroline's apartment for a few days until we see which way the wind blows." He didn't give either of them time to respond and just left the room, shutting the door behind him.

"He's kinda intense."

"Yeah, Beautiful." Rory turned to the single window in the room and pulled back the blind, peering out. "Intense is in his DNA, I think."

"His wife deserves a medal for putting up with him."

Rory snorted out loud. "Dalton putting up with Lina or Lina putting up with Dalton? Ha, it's a toss-up between which of them deserves that medal. His wife, Lina, is just as bad as he is."

"It must make it awkward to be around them." She was always fascinated by the dynamics of people and relationships.

"Nah. They spark off each other like it's going out of

style. But there is nobody else for the boss but his princess, and nobody for Lina but her sailor."

"They are lucky." Envy had a color, just like everyone said. However, the green wasn't a muted sage color, it was a bright Kelly green. "Most people search for that for a lifetime."

"They do," Rory agreed with her. "They haven't had it easy. There's been more than a little war, a couple of kidnappings, assassins, and a marriage that was sorta kinda fake."

She already knew about the troubles Eedana had when she'd first met Logan and had heard some of Cormack's wife, Willow's, story. "I'm starting to think any woman who comes near you people and hears the trauma the women go through should just turn around on their heels and nope right on out of that situation."

"Is that what you want to do about this?" He waved a hand back and forth between them. "Nope out of the situation?"

"Ah, but we aren't in a relationship."

"Are you sure about that?"

Up until this point she had assumed he was rather intelligent. She was swiftly reevaluating that opinion. "I—"

"We're back." Snow swept into the room and dropped the shopping bags on the bed next to Adalyn. "Move your ass, Mokaccino. I need to help your woman get dressed."

He nodded to them both and left the room.

CHAPTER EIGHT

"I can walk, you know." Why the heck did hospitals always want you to sit in a wheelchair to leave? As if you hadn't been confined enough for however long your stay was. Although, to be fair, with the way Rory was zooming her down corridors and around corners with the rest of his team flanking them, she must seem like either a prisoner or celebrity to anyone seeing her.

"I know." Rory pushed the chair. "Look, no hands."

"Jeez, Mokaccino, what the hell are you doing?" She thought this might be Jeep who she'd been introduced to as they'd left her room a few minutes before. "Do not drop her out of the chair or she'll be staying here until she recovers."

"Yes, please don't do that." Adalyn wrapped her fingers around the arms of the wheelchair. "I don't want to stay here while you search for Sam." Did they not realize how much breathing hurt? Or how absolutely terrified she was that she'd never find her son?

Is trusting these people the wrong thing to do?
How do I know they can find him?
Why haven't the French police come and asked me questions?

Why aren't they looking for my son?

She had a billion and one questions and no answers. Most of the team left to go grab the cars. "Rory?"

"Yes, Beautiful?"

"Promise me we will find him."

"I swear it." Rory came around to the front of the wheelchair and crouched down on his haunches. "We will find him. I won't stop until we do."

Her heart was torn in two. God help her, she wanted so badly to believe him, but she'd read the news enough and had gone down way too many rabbit holes on the dark web for research for her storylines that she knew the realities of her situation. So many parents never got the outcome they wanted.

"Hey." Rory cupped her cheek with his hand. "I swear we will never stop looking. Nemesis will burn the world to the ground to find your son. I swear it." He glanced over his shoulder as a line of black SUVs came to a stop in front of them. "I'm going to pick you up," he warned her. "If I hurt you, tell me, and we'll figure out another way."

She nodded in reply as there wasn't any chance she was going to be able to voice her agreement. Not with a lump the size of a fireside log lodged in her throat. The cry of pain that had no such sensibilities escaped.

"Shit."

"It's going to hurt, no matter how we get me out of this chair." It wasn't exactly reassuring, but it was the best she could do. "Either you pull me to my feet or you pick me up, but decide please."

He nodded and lifted her up, then turned and slid them into the car with her on his lap. "We aren't risking a seat belt, but I'll keep you safe," he promised.

Adalyn moved carefully, adjusting herself on his lap and settling against his chest. It was ridiculous how comfortable she'd become around him in the last day and a half since he'd swept into her room. "Mmh."

"You okay there, Beautiful?"

"Yes." She winced as the SUV went over a speed bump in the street.

"Sorry," Dalton called over his shoulder. "I didn't see that one. I'll try and be more careful. The damn bumps are the same color as the asphalt."

"It's okay. I know you didn't do it on purpose."

"He better not have," Rory whispered against her head. She was guessing nobody else was meant to hear it, but when Logan snickered next to them, she was guessing he had picked up on it.

"Where are we going?"

"To a safe house."

"An apartment which belongs to a friend of my wife's." Dalton eased them to a stop at traffic lights. "It's a ball-ache to get to, but it has parking, and we'll have space to leave your van there if we find it."

She nodded in response. She'd written about safe houses often enough that she understood the concept. It was kind of exciting to finally get to see one.

"Won't be long," Logan chimed in. "It's in the city center, right, Boss?"

"Yup, prime real estate."

She moved with the motion of the car in the safety of Rory's arms as they went around a roundabout, and straightened again without doing herself an injury, only to brace herself against the seat in front of her when Dalton slammed on the brakes to avoid a pair of bicycles.

"Fuckers. You don't own the road!" Dalton yelled. "Next time I'll make you a stain for the street cleaners to clean up."

"Well, that's a colorful way to put it."

"These assholes think they own the fucking streets, and I

can't even blow them out of it with the horn because I don't want to draw attention to us," Dalton grumbled.

"Is this an 'I *need* pops situation'?" She wasn't entirely sure of the dynamics of the team yet, but normally she was pretty fast on the uptake and once she didn't hurt quite so much, she would figure them out.

"Nah, Beautiful, this is nothing. Just a normal day at the office when Nemesis is behind the wheel."

"I think this is us up here, Boss." Logan glanced up from his phone where he was studying Google Maps. "GPS lady appears to be on strike so she's saying jack."

As if to make a complete and utter liar out of him, his phone cackled into life. *Make a U-turn.*

"What?"

Make a U-turn.

"Is GPS lady fucking insane?" Dalton asked. "Where the fuck does she want me to make a U-turn? Into the fucking hotel right there?"

Turn left.

"That's The Seine, Boss; do not turn left," Rory advised.

"Do you think I'm fucking dense? Of course I'm not going to turn left into The Fucking Seine."

Should she tell them now that GPS didn't work in Paris at all, or was it better to let this play out and see what happened? But if it played out and she had to laugh, it was going to hurt like a mother-trucker on crack. She opened her mouth and shut it again when GPS lady got there before she did.

At the next roundabout, take the second exit.

"Second exit, Boss," Logan called.

"Got it." He slowed down, not quite coming to a stop before nosing the SUV into the roundabout. "One... fuck, was that two or three?" Dalton took the next exit.

Make a U-turn.

Recalculating route.
Make a U-turn.

"Wrong exit, Boss."

"Fuuuuck."

"Calm down, Boss." Rory's voice rumbled in his chest as she rested against it. Adalyn gave up trying to brace herself against seats and such and let Rory do all the work. It didn't hurt her as much that way. "You're slamming on brakes and shit and Adalyn's hurt."

"Sorry." Dalton tapped the brakes, slowing them down again. "Where is the next exit so we can get back into town?"

Adalyn grinned when all three men ducked as the SUV drove into a tunnel. "I think this might be where Princess Diana was killed."

"I do not need to hear that." Dalton scowled. "Do not talk of dying when we're in tunnels, jeez."

"He's freaking as he hates not knowing where he's going and GPS lady stressed him out."

Turn right.

"It's a fucking tunnel."

Searching for route.
Make a U-turn.
Searching for route.

"Turn that fucking bitch off and get me Trev on the line," Dalton ordered. "Now, Sensei."

"Yes, Sir." Logan pressed buttons on his phone.

Make a U-tu—

GPS lady was cut off and the sound of a call connecting came over the speaker phone.

"TOC, here."

"Tock?"

"Tactical operations center."

"Oh, I should have known that. It was part of my research for a book last year."

"This whole scene is going to make it into a book, isn't it?" Rory whispered.

"Damn straight," she whispered back. "It's too funny not to." She giggled. "The big bad operator driven to insanity by three words. Make a U-turn."

"Make a U-turn."

They grinned at each other.

"Jinx."

"Jinx." She smiled up at him. "See, you're learning."

"Shut the fuck up!" Dalton yelled. "I can't hear what TOC is saying and I'm driving us toward fucking Germany or something."

"Sorry, Boss."

Her ears picked up at Dalton's order, and she turned to look out the windows, trying to see if she recognized any landmarks. There was that auto shop with the huge pink flamingo she'd driven past it on the way to the store with Sam.

"Rory?"

"Yes, Beautiful?"

"How do we make him stop?"

"The man who took you and find Sam?"

"No, him. Dalton."

"What?" Dalton looked quickly over his shoulder and immediately turned back to watch where he was going. "Are you going to be sick?"

"No, but…"

"Tell me." Rory gently tipped up her chin to look into her eyes. "I'm listening."

"I think we're near where Sam and I was taken from."

"Boss, TOC," the man on the phone interrupted. "Rory's lady is right. According to the police reports I found, the store is about two miles north from your position."

"Gimme the directions."

"Keep going straight until you come to the exit for Paris city center, and it's the second of two exits," Adalyn answered. "Make sure you take the second one, as the first leads you into where a derelict mall is. I made that mistake the other day." She sighed as he took the exit she'd just told him not to take. "And he took it anyway."

"Ha." Rory snorted.

"Wrong exit, Mr. Nemesis."

"Fuck." Dalton slowed the SUV again. If they were driving any slower at this point, they'd be stopped.

"If you go all the way down to the end of this road, there's a roundabout." She gave him the directions she'd used last time. But as they neared the roundabout, she saw a flash of blue out of the corner of her eye. "Sally, oh my God, there's Sally. STOP."

"What the hell?" Dalton slammed on the brakes, both of his hands wrapped so tightly around the steering wheel she could see the whites of his knuckles. "Who the fuck is Sally?"

"My van." Every ache, pain, scratch, cut, and bruise was forgotten in her excitement, and she bounced on Rory's lap. Reality slammed into her as her throat closed and her eyes filled with tears. "Oh my God, please. Sam might be in there. We have to look. Please. Please."

"Keep your pants on, I'm going." Dalton took the first exit at the roundabout. "How the fuck have the cops not found this? Did they even look? Jesus."

"Boss, TOC, will I alert the relevant authorities?"

"Go ahead, TOC." Dalton pulled his SUV to a stop out of sight of the van and the others behind them followed suit. "But you also tell them I'm not waiting to check it. Give them my NATO and Interpol ID and clearances."

"On it, Sir," Trev said. "TOC out."

"You stay in the SUV," Dalton ordered. "We approach as a team."

"I'm coming to—"

"Hell fucking no!" Rory yelled, then softened his tone. "We work as a team; we train for this. Let us do our jobs."

"But Sam might be in—"

"And if he is, you endanger him by wanting to be there," Rory said. "This is our jam, our specialty is HVT recovery, and trust me, there is no higher value target for us right now than your son."

The momma bear inside her didn't want to listen to him. She wanted to argue. But every minute they waited was a minute wasted. "There is a spare key under the wheel arch on the back driver's side."

"Good girl, Beautiful." Rory kissed the top off her head and exited the SUV. "Stay here with everything locked. We'll be a few minutes."

"Okay."

The rear door of the SUV was opened, and within minutes she hardly recognized any of the team. They wore tactical vests, headgear, earpieces, and all the other equipment she wrote about. The phone was laid on the back of the SUV, and Trev in TOC sent them a map of the area. Within fifteen minutes they were armed to the teeth and had a plan in place.

Rory leaned in the door. "Come here, Beautiful." He helped her out of the back and led her around to the driver's door. "You wait here. If anyone but us approaches, you put this puppy in drive and take off all the while laying on the horn so we know you need backup, got it?"

"Yes." More than anything she wanted to be right there with them. But she also wasn't stupid. In her condition she'd slow them down and possibly put Sam in danger. "Be safe."

Rory nodded, turned away, and fell into formation with his team. She watched them as they moved as one unit until they disappeared around the corner and out of view.

"Please, God. Please, I'll do anything. Have Sam be there and be okay." All she could do now was wait and pray for everyone's safety, but most of all that of her son. The next few minutes were going to be the longest ones of her life and there was absolutely nothing she could do about it.

"How are you doing there, Ms. Cassidy?"

"Eeeeep." She screeched when a voice spoke from the passenger seat and jumped high enough to hit her stomach off the steering wheel as she jerked away from it.

"I'm sorry, it's Trev in TOC," the voice explained. "This is Mokaccino's phone. If you need something, holler, and I'll let them know."

She pressed her hand into her chest, using the pain it caused her aching ribs to remind herself that she hadn't had a heart attack from the shock. "Next time, remind him to tell me he's leaving his phone," she said. "You scared the shit out of me."

"Yes, Ma'am."

"Now focus on them and my van."

"Yes, Ma'am," Trev replied. "TOC ou—"

"Trev?"

"Yes, Ma'am?"

"Will you tell me if Sam is there?"

"Yes, Ma'am, as soon as I have clearance to do so."

"Thank you." It was the best she could hope for at this point.

"TOC, out," Trev said. Before the line went quiet, she heard him say, "Three, two, one, execute. Execute. Execute."

"Oh." This time, rather than pray out loud, now that she had an audience she kept her prayers to herself.

Please, God, let Sam be there.

Please keep everyone safe.

CHAPTER NINE

"TOC, One." Dalton was just a couple of steps ahead of him, but when he spoke, Rory heard his words softly through his earpiece rather than out loud. "How are we looking?"

"One, TOC," Trev replied. "I can't see any movement. Everything looks clear. I'm just going to try and get a better angle on this satellite, but it's set up for Google Maps, so it's not Navy awesome."

"Roger." Dalton clicked on the device and continued, "Want me to give them some movement and see if it gives you anything?"

"Good thinking," Trev replied. "On my count. Three, two, one, go."

Dalton sidestepped out of cover with his weapon at ready position and Cormack on his six, keeping him covered.

"Retreat," Trev ordered after about a minute. "No movement from our target zone. It looks dead over there."

Rory's heart stuttered in his chest. Fuck, he really hoped that little boy wasn't dead in the van they readied to approach. It would destroy Adalyn.

And you.

Yes, and him. He could admit that to himself. He may have never met Sam, but everything in him wanted that to be possible. It had to be possible. Anything else was unthinkable. A hand touched him lightly on the shoulder and he glanced back at Logan. He glanced at Logan's thumbs up and gave a short nod.

Yes, I'm good.

He forced everything but the job to come out of his head. Feelings and emotions were for after the job was done. He went through his usual routine. Check his comms, touch where his flash bangs hung on his belt, and check the safety was disengaged on his weapon.

"All Stations, TOC," Trev said, and Rory tensed. This was it, go time. "Three, two, one, execute. Execute. Execute."

They moved at a crouched run across the parking lot to where the van was parked and slid in next to it, making sure to keep themselves under the windows. Rory ended up next to the rear wheel and he reached underneath the arch, searching for the spare key Adalyn had said was there. His fingers closed around a box which felt very similar to the one he'd found under his rented SUV when he'd touched down in Paris a couple of days ago. He pulled it free and winced when his diver's watch snagged against the edge of the metal, making a soft clanging noise.

Jeep tapped him on the shoulder and Rory handed the box to him. His part was done until the doors were open. Jeep opened the box and extracted the key, then handed it to Dalton to insert it in the lock. Hopefully, the locking mechanism was well oiled and wasn't loud as it unlocked. They had decided to use the key to ensure the alarm system was disengaged to avoid alerting anyone inside the van of their presence.

The two seconds it took for Dalton to insert the key and turn it took what felt like an hour, but all he could do was suck it up and deal. As soon as they heard the click, the whole team exploded into action.

Rory stepped around the side of the van with Logan joining him from the opposite side. Logan wrapped his fingers into the handle and yanked open the doors as Dalton and Snow did the same with the front doors.

His eyes widened when he was met with a queen-sized bed and not the open back of a van. Adalyn had said she and Sam lived in the van but the mechanics of that hadn't occurred to him. His eyes searched the interior of the van. "Clear."

"Clear."

"Clear."

Fuck. Sam's not here.

"Boss," Snow called from her side of the van. "You need to see this."

Rory's heart sank. He could tell by the sound of Snow's voice that what she'd found wasn't good. He couldn't see a fucking thing from his position. "Stay here," he ordered Logan, and once he confirmed he had this side covered, he rounded the rear of the van to the passenger sliding door just in time to see Dalton curse viciously, turn away, and punch a nearby tree.

"Is it Sam?"

Snow put her hands on his chest, pushing him back. "You don't need to see this, Rory," she said softly.

He wrapped his hands around her wrists and made her move. "I have to."

"Ro—"

Snow calling him by his first name and not his call sign should have been his third clue, her tone when she'd called Dalton the first, and Dalton punching the tree the second. Yet the sight which greeted him on the floor of the van brought him to his knees. Written in what suspiciously like blood were five words.

The kid for the Mamba.

Rory's breath sawed in and out of his chest as he fought for air. "Fuck. Fuck. Fuck."

"It's not a body," Snow reminded him. "There's still hope when there's no body."

"Sam in exchange for Lina." Now he understood why Dalton was furious. His pregnant wife in exchange for an innocent little boy. Essentially putting two babies in the palm of King, because it had to be the Organization. "How do I tell Adalyn?"

"I don't know." Snow helped him to his feet. "I don't know."

"Six, TOC," Trev hailed him over comms. "I have advised your lady that her son is not present."

"Thank you, TOC." That wasn't what he was struggling with. How the hell did he tell Adalyn that there was no way in hell Dalton was going to exchange his wife and child for her son?

"We'll figure out a way." Jeep nudged him back from the van. "I hear sirens, so the police are on the way. We don't want to fuck up any evidence they might find, so don't touch anything."

"Yeah."

"All Stations. TOC, confirmation the authorities are coming in hot. Retreat to vehicles and de-weaponize yourselves."

"Copy that."

"Aye," Dalton agreed. "Fall in, team."

There was nothing for Rory to do but what he was told. He stepped into his position and moved with his team back across the lot and around the side of the building to where they'd stashed the SUVs and Adalyn.

Even though Trev had told Adalyn her son wasn't in the van, Rory could see her searching each and every one of their faces, looking for any hint or indication of what they'd found. She flicked her gaze over the others, but even through the blacked-out windows of the SUV he could make out when she locked onto him, and he felt her disappointment down to his toes.

"I'll deal with the cops." Dalton pushed a piece of paper and a set of keys into his hand. "This is the address of the safe house. Be gone before the cops pull in here."

"Yes, Sir." He rounded the hood to the driver's side of the SUV and opened the door. "We need to move fast, Beautiful. Let's get you situated, and I'll fill you in when we get to the house." He almost carried her to the back seat and settled her in. "You'll have to wear a belt." He grabbed it from behind her and clipped it closed. "I'll try not to hurt you as we try to get out of here before the French authorities get here. You'll have to man GPS until Trev can help us out in a few minutes."

"I could sit in the passenger—"

He slammed the door shut and got into the front. "No time, Beautiful." He gunned the engine and drove them around the back of the mall parking lot. "Sorry." He apologized for his abruptness. "But unless you want to be stuck here for hours dealing with more police questions, then it's better we go fast." He tried to ease the SUV over a speed bump but knew it was still too rough when she gasped behind him.

"Just drive. I'm okay."

Every second he spent with her, she impressed him more and more. He knew a hell of a lot of men who would be curled up in a corner bawling their eyes out at the pain she must be in, yet here she was trying to keep him from seeing that she was hurting.

"You need to go straight through at these lights."

"Where's GPS lady?"

"Drinking somewhere," she said. "It's better if I just get us back to where we went wrong the last time."

"Do you know where we are going?"

"No."

He tossed the paper over his shoulder. "That's the address, put it in the phone so it shows you where we need to go at least."

"I feel like I should toss out a snappy 'yes, Sir' here."

He'd come to realize that throwing down a snarky or somewhat amusing comment was her way of keeping herself from freaking out. He could totally deal with that. It sure beat tears and a meltdown like his sisters would be doing right about now. "Ha."

"Do you want to try GPS again?" she asked. "Or do you want me to just read the map?"

"Can you read a map?"

"The phone is giving me the route." In the rearview mirror, he could see her dragging her fingers on the screen as if she was zooming in. "I can tell you left or right, but if you're looking for east or west, I'm totally not your girl."

"Left or right works." There was no way he was telling her he needed a left or a right when driving too.

"You might want to change lanes, as we're going right after this exit."

"Got it." He flipped on his blinker and eased into the tiny gap between a semi and a smart car. "Next right, yeah?"

"Yes, please, then stay to the left. That will take us back under the tunnel again."

"Okay."

Somehow, working together they managed to make it through Paris traffic and to the door of an underground parking lot.

"This is it, right?"

RORY

"I think so." He twisted in his seat. "Is there a code on that paper?"

"Five, six, one, zero, four, hash."

Rory lowered the window and leaned out. "Five, six, one…"

"Zero, four, hash."

The lights on either side of the door flashed yellow and it slowly opened, revealing an unlit parking lot with space for about ten vehicles.

"Is there a number on the apartment?"

"Ten."

"The guys can figure out where they are putting their trucks. I'm parking in number ten. It's closer to the elevator so you won't have to walk as far."

"Thank you."

He pulled into the spot and stopped the SUV. "Stay there a second. I need to stash some of this gear and my weapon. If someone sees me armed to the teeth, we'll open a can of worms which should stay shut."

"Of course."

He grabbed his M-16 and unclipped it from the strap which he had secured it to his vest. He rounded the SUV and opened the trunk and located the secure lock box he knew he'd find there. After pulling off his armor, he secured it and his long gun, then snagged a sidearm and shoulder holster. He didn't want to have to rely on only his knives if there were any problems. Especially not with Adalyn to protect. He glanced over the back seat to see her watching him, her eyes wary. "Do my weapons bother you?"

"No." She shook her head. "I grew up around weapons; it's just unusual to see them over here."

"Yeah, it's a good thing nobody spotted them while we were driving, or they'd have reported it." He snapped the lid of the lockbox shut and spun the dials to lock it. "That's a whole lot of paperwork Dalton would be thrilled to deal with." He slammed the trunk shut and opened the passenger door for her. "Ready?"

"Yes." She allowed him to help her out of the SUV and into the elevator. "Top floor is ten." She hit the button and nothing happened. The doors didn't even close. "Is there a key?"

"I don't see where we would put a key." He ran his hand all over the dark wood looking for a keyhole and didn't find one. Then he started pressing all the other buttons. "Does it work for any other floor?"

"Apparently not." She squeezed her eyes shut and breathed out a long slow breath as if she were psyching herself up for the trek. "I guess we're taking the stairs."

"Yeah." He took her hand in his and led her out of the elevator. "Just our luck that the elevator isn't working."

As they approached the door to the stairway, he opened it and held it open with his back. "I'll carry you up."

"I'm too heavy for you to carry me up ten flights of stairs."

"Stop it." Careful of not hurting her, he tugged her to a stop. "Do you not realize that I call you 'Beautiful' because you are?"

"No, I'm…"

He stopped her denial in the only way he could think of. He kissed her. His lips stroking across hers, once, twice, three times, careful of the sore spot from the split on the side. This wasn't the raw steaming hot kiss he couldn't wait to give her when she was recovered, if she'd let him. This one was soft, gentle, and its effect slammed into his heart like nothing ever had before.

CHAPTER TEN

Adalyn winced when Rory's hand tugged her to a stop, twisting her torso in the process. She bit down on her sore lips to ensure she didn't cry out in pain. He'd been so kind to her, and she just knew he'd be so mad with himself if he knew he'd caused her pain.

"Do you not realize that I call you 'Beautiful' because you are?"

"No, I'm…" Had he not seen the state of her face? The rest of her wasn't any great beautiful sight either. She was bruised and battered like a linebacker after Saturday night's football game. Plus, she wasn't exactly tiny. She spent way more time sitting on her butt writing stories than she did exercising. Even if her last round of tests when she'd purchased her travel health insurance had put her healthy as a horse, there was at least thirty pounds which she should be making a priority to take off but just couldn't bring herself to worry too much about it. Until now, when he said he wanted to carry her up ten freaking flights of stairs.

Her eyes widened as he lowered her mouth toward her. She blinked and stared, watching as he moved as if in slow motion.

When his lips brushed over hers, she sighed and his groan in response to the sound sent goose bumps racing along her skin.

Wow—um—wow.

Her sore fingers wrapped into his shirt and she tugged him closer, stepping onto her tippy toes to kiss him again.

His mouth brushed over a sore spot, and she wanted to kick her own butt for wincing as he pulled back. They stared at each other for a couple of heartbeats and then the guilt slammed into her.

What the hell were you thinking?

Sam. Is. Missing.

Missing.

And you are here locking lips with Captain America.

Are you crazy?

"Stop." Rory ran one finger lightly down her cheek. "You are not a horrible person for seeking comfort—or taking it once it's offered."

Comfort.

It's comfort.

Okay.

Okay.

He sighed deeply and scooped her into his arms before she could open her mouth to protest again and muttered, "Don't, just don't."

She swallowed down the protest and let him have his way. It was silly to think she had hurt him. But it kind of felt like she had. She just couldn't figure out how or why.

"I think this is us." Rory carefully lowered her to her feet in front of a black door with number ten in silver letters on it. He took the keys from her and pushed the big one in the lock, turned before doing the same with the smaller key in the deadbolt lock above it, and pushed open the door.

She frowned in confusion when he stopped her from

entering the apartment and pulled his handgun from the holster he'd put on at the car. Understanding dawned; he wanted to sweep the apartment first.

I wonder what he'd do if I handed him a broom for that?

But instead of snickering at the thought, she kept her face passive and nodded that she understood.

"Stay right behind me," Rory whispered. "I don't want you to stay out here by yourself but bringing you in here without clearing it first makes my skin crawl. Please make sure your eyes are on me at all times."

"Okay." She could do that. It couldn't be that difficult to walk right behind his extremely fine butt.

He didn't say to keep your eyes on his butt the whole time.

It would be tragic not to.

Sam.

The unofficial horrible mother of the year award went to her. She kept as close to his heels as she could without tripping over him. It would be just her luck to step on him just as someone jumped out of the stunningly ornate armoire across the room.

They went through the apartment room by room and ended up back in the living room.

"We're good." Rory quirked up the corner of his lip. "If someone is hiding under the bed, then they are about two inches tall, and probably covered in dust."

"It's a shame to see this beautiful room not being looked after." There was no way they would be able to sit down on the couch until they'd at least run the vacuum and pulled off all the dust cloths covering the furniture.

"The lady, Caroline, who owns this place is in the hospital," Rory reminded her. "She has been for weeks. From what the boss says, her family isn't exactly the run over and water your plants type."

"I know. Help me pull off these dust cloths and we'll get to work."

"You aren't cleaning." He pointed a single finger at her. "I am. You're hurt."

"If I'm not too hurt for kissing, then I'm not too hurt for cleaning."

"Big difference between kissing and cleaning." He leaned his face in close to hers and whispered the words in her ear, sending a shiver down her spine. "Big. Big. Difference."

"If you say so." She turned her head to look at him, their lips almost brushing together but not quite.

"I do."

He cleared his throat, and she ripped her gaze away from him, stepping back and putting a couple of more inches between them. "I'll—uh—get the drop cloths." He reached down, grabbed a fist full of the material, and pulled, sending a cloud of dust swirling around them.

She could feel the sneeze coming. Her throat tickled and her nose twitched. "Shit." She wrapped her arm around her rib cage, trying to hold her sore spots so they wouldn't hurt quite so much. "Achoo. Mother-trucker, that hurts."

"Fuck, I'm so sorry." Rory bundled up the drop cloth. "I didn't think." He dropped it in the corner. "Are you okay? Can I…"

"Don't touch me." This was how she was going to die. With her ribs broken from a sneeze. It had to be. "Just don't touch me, fudge—freaking—crapola—mother—freaking—trucker—ow—just—ow."

"I'm sorry," Rory repeated. "So fucking sorry. I didn't think the dust would cloud up like that. I'm calling the boss; we can't stay here."

"No." She leaned a hand on the back of the cloth-covered ladder-back chair next to what she thought was a dining table. She didn't dare breathe through her mouth. If she sneezed again, she was going to freaking cry and he didn't need to see that. Crying was something she didn't like anyone to see her do. Because if you looked up ugly crying in the dictionary, you would find a picture of her with her nose as red as Rudolph's, swollen eyes, and blotchy skin. "No, don't call him. I'll be okay in a minute."

"I—"

"I promise, I'll be fine." She'd done childbirth, she could do hurt ribs too.

"Then come into the kitchen; nothing is covered there so hopefully it won't be so bad."

"Go in and check. I'll be in in a minute."

He studied her for a second, as if trying to decide if she was going to fall over the second he turned his back, but thankfully, he nodded and turned away. Once the door swung shut behind him, she braced herself on the back of the chair and dropped her head as low as she could without it hurting. "Shit, ow, fuck, shit." Now that she was on her own, she could swear freely.

"Fuck."

His swearing had her straightening painfully. He came running out of the kitchen and she braced herself to run with him.

"What's wrong?"

He glanced toward the apartment door and back again, twice, clearly undecided on what he should do.

"Rory?" She snapped out his name, just as she would with Sam when she needed his attention immediately. "What's wrong?"

"King." He pulled his phone out of his pocket and scrolled through the screens.

"King?"

"Someone the boss has been hunting a long time. I just

saw him on the street below." He put the cell to his ear. "If it was just me, I'd follow him."

She plucked the phone out of his hand. "Go. I'll lock the door behind you." She glanced at the phone. "But you didn't press call on this."

"Hit redial, it rang out." Rory was clearly hesitant to leave her on her own. "And of course the boss doesn't have a voice mail set up. I'll call Trev."

"Go, follow your King. I'm fine. Nobody knows I'm here."

"I—"

"The longer you wait, the further away he's getting. Go."

"Do not answer the door for anyone but me," he ordered. "I don't care if it's the boss, nobody but me…got it?"

"Yes, I got it."

"If he doesn't answer, press speed dial one. It will get you through to Trev in our head office. Tell him what's happening."

"Okay, I can do that. Go." She followed him to the door and ushered him through it. She shut it and turned both the key and the deadbolt, ensuring it was locked behind him. Thankfully the phone hadn't locked itself and she went into the previously dialed numbers, hit redial, and put it to her ear. After about four rings the tone in her ear changed, but the call was almost immediately answered before she could figure out what was happening.

"Go for TOC."

"Um." Crapola, she hadn't thought about what she was going to say when the call was answered. Usually, she rehearsed what she wanted to say multiple times before actually hitting call. "Ah—um—this is Adalyn—" Lovely; she sounded like a bumbling idiot.

"Is Mokaccino down?" She could hear the concern in Trev's voice. "I—"

"No, wait. He's not, um, down." *I'm an author, y'all, I work with words, and apparently can't even string a sentence together today.* "At least I don't think so."

"He's not with you?" Trev asked. "Where the hell is he?"

"Following someone called King."

"Repeat that!" Trev snapped out the order.

"He saw someone called King, and I made him go after him when he said his boss was chasing him." It probably had been a stupid move to encourage him to go. She had to work harder than she would like to keep herself calm. "It seemed stupid to sit here watching me when it was someone he was clearly itching to follow," she explained lamely. Finding Sam and her own safety should be her first priority. "In my defense, my brain isn't exactly in perfect working order."

"Clearly, Costa's isn't either," Trev muttered. "Stay put, keep the doors locked. I'll have someone with you in a couple of minutes."

"I'm not opening the door to anyone but Rory," she replied. "I promised."

"Good. They can wait outside the door," Trev said. "I'll be back, keep this phone on."

"Okay." The phone went dead in her ear, and she placed it on the table. She glanced around the dusty room. If she could find some cleaning products, she could make a start on cleaning. That would keep her brain busy and hopefully help with the freakout she could feel building inside her. She double-checked the door was locked again, then turned toward the kitchen. Hopefully little old French ladies kept their cleaning products under the sink too.

CHAPTER ELEVEN

Rory waited to hear the sounds of the locks engaging on the apartment door before he bolted toward the stairs. Hopefully, King would still be somewhere in sight by the time he made it down to the street. But he couldn't count on it. He hesitated at the door to check his weapon and scan the street ahead of him. He had no comms, no phone, and no way of getting in touch with anyone if the shit hit the fan. "Boss will just have to give me double PT or some shit," he decided. Finding King and leads to The Organization had been priority number one for months, but now the possibility the fucking bastard had Sam, it was too tempting to not follow him. If he got in shit for following up a lead, so be it. He slipped his weapon back into its holster and stepped out onto the street.

Where are you, asswipe?

He searched the people on the street ahead of him, looking for the pale gray suit King had been wearing when he'd spotted him a few minutes ago. Walking down the street attempting to look normal while you were looking for someone wasn't always the easiest feat. But in a city like

Paris, where the streets were full of tourists, it was slightly easier. Every gray suit wearing man got a second look, but damn it, none of them were the man he was looking for.

King had to be somewhere. This wasn't an episode of *Ghostbusters*, and people didn't just disappear into thin air. Ahead of him on the opposite side of the street he spotted a hotel. Wasn't that the chain Trev had mentioned when they'd been searching for Lina all those months ago? He reached for his cell to double-check and silently swore in his head; he'd given it to Adalyn. "I should have kept my comms unit, damn it." Muttering quietly under his breath, he stopped at a pedestrian crossing and waited for the little red man to turn green before crossing the street. "There you are." Ahead of him at the next set of lights, he spotted King sidestepping around a man before climbing the steps to the hotel. "Got you."

As if King heard his whisper, the man spun around to glance up and down the street. Rory paused and glanced in the window of a pastry shop, trying to look like a tourist trying to decide what he would like to try. In the reflection, he could just about make out King's outline as he went in through the hotel doors.

Now he had a decision to make: go back to the apartment and grab his phone and get orders from Dalton, or he could waltz his happy ass right on into that hotel and plant it somewhere he could keep an eye on King.

Adalyn will have called Dalton. He'll know I'm tracking King.

It would be fucking awesome to have King in sight when Dalton found him. He had no doubt Dalton would find him. It was why every member of Nemesis had trackers embedded in their skin. Trev had been intrigued by the tracker Dalton had dug out of Lina's butt and decided it was something Nemesis should implement. Rory's was embedded in his chest, just under where his dog tags rested against his skin. Should he be scanned, it was hoped any beep would be assumed to be caused by the metal of his tags.

Rory strolled down the street and into the hotel before taking a seat in the small bar area which gave him full view of the foyer. "One coffee, please," he asked the waitress loudly. Sometimes play the loud brash American tourist was the best way to hide in plain sight. Most Europeans wouldn't pay much attention to another loud American.

"Of course, Monsieur."

He scanned the bar area, disappointed when he didn't see his target. Hopefully, King wasn't just using this hotel as a pass-through location and was somewhere still in the building. He swept his eyes around the room again and glanced at the revolving door when it turned once again.

"Shit," he whispered softly when the door spat out Dalton. Rory glanced over his boss's shoulder, expecting to see more of their team on his six, and frowned when the door stopped turning.

This can't be his plan.

Fuck.

Is he insane?

The answer to that question he knew was, yes, yes, Dalton was partially insane. Hell, anyone who worked in this business for long enough probably was a touch insane. But walking into a hotel where King was suspected to be was more insane than usual, even for Nemesis.

He scanned Dalton from head to toe. Instead of the black tactical clothes he wore earlier, now he wore a smart suit. Knowing Dalton and his family money, that suit probably cost more money than Rory made in a month. He could tell by the fit of his jacket, Dalton carried no weapons. At least, he didn't carry a sidearm that Rory could see. Blades and some throwing stars were a given; his boss never went anywhere without at least a couple of each.

"What the fuck, Mokaccino?" Dalton pulled out a chair on the opposite side of the table to him and sat with his back to the door, which Rory knew was only possible because the mirror behind him gave Dalton a clear view of anyone approaching behind him. "Has every single brain cell you have migrated to your balls?"

"No, Sir." He leaned back to make room for the waitress to place his coffee in front of him. "May we have another coffee for my friend please?"

"Of course, Monsieur." The waitress smiled at him. "I'll be back in just a moment."

"I figured you would want to know who I saw."

"Trev told me." Dalton looked past Rory's left ear, clearly watching the mirror. "That's the only reason I'm not causing a scene and dragging you out of here by the ears. But we'll discuss that later." He glanced up at the waitress. "Thank you, Ma'am."

"You're welcome, Sir." The waitress left, pausing at the table next to them to load up her tray before going back to the bar counter.

"Adalyn?"

"Jeep has her."

Relief he hadn't expected to feel swept through him, and he ruthlessly pushed it aside. Jeep being with Adalyn also explained why their second in command wasn't right here on Dalton's heels keeping him out of trouble.

"Where is he?"

"He came in here," Rory said softly. "But I haven't seen him since I got here."

"Okay." Dalton shrugged as if he didn't give a shit, but Rory knew that was a lie.

"There's one camera over the bar, trained on the front door," Rory informed him and gave a run-down of all the features he'd logged in his head during his sweep of the room just before Dalton had entered. "Another over the exit to what looks like the John."

"Got them."

"The dude behind the bar is armed, as are the two men next to the reception desk."

"Hotel security in Paris isn't typically armed, unless they have someone really important on site."

"Agree." And despite the name he used, King was as far from royalty as you could get. Unless you counted fucked up underworld royalty. Rory tensed at the sound of a phone ringing toward the bar. Over Dalton's shoulder, both armed men who had stood near the reception desk approached. "Incoming," he warned softly.

"I see them." Dalton lounged back in his chair and stretched one leg out in front of him, as if he didn't have a care in the world. "Kiss it, Mokaccino."

Fuck.

Keep it simple, stupid.

In other words... follow his boss's lead.

He gave a short nod in response. *Yes.*

"Excuse me, Sirs." The two men paused at either side of Dalton. The one who spoke did so in a middle eastern accent. "The hotel owner requests the pleasure of your presence in his office, Mr. Knight."

There was the confirmation King knew exactly who Dalton was. Not that Rory had expected any different, given the history between the two men.

"Does he now?" Dalton raised one eyebrow. "And tell me, gentlemen, why I should care what your boss wants?"

The first man tensed, but the second reached under his suit jacket with one hand. Rory and Dalton exchanged glances. Words weren't needed.

Dalton moved his eyes to the left in a silent order. *"Wait."*

RORY

"Copy that." Rory rubbed two fingers on the tip of his nose.

"When Mr. King requests your presence, your response is always, 'of course, lead the way.'"

"No." Dalton picked up the coffee mug and put it to his lips, even though Rory knew there was no way in hell he would drink from it. Having a wife who specialized in poison was a surefire way to remind a man of the dangers of drinking or eating in places where you suspected you were hated with the vengeance of a thousand Mongols headed for China. "If your Mr. King wants to speak to me, he can present his pompous ass here in front of me. Otherwise, my friend and I are done here." Dalton scooted back his chair, putting himself between the two men.

Rory got to his feet at the same time. "I would advise you not to tou—" The idiots obviously didn't care what he'd been about to advise them, as both reached for Dalton. "Fools."

Dalton's fists closed; he swung his arms forward and slammed his elbows back into the stomachs of both men, doubling them over. People exclaimed in surprise as Dalton slammed the face of one off the table and punched the other, flattening him on his back. "Let's go."

"You didn't leave anything for me to do," Rory complained as he stepped over the two men in Dalton's wake. "Boss, you aren't meant to have all the fun yourself." His snark and bullshit were a way to cover how he scanned the bar and the foyer on the way to the door.

"Tell your boss I only do visits when I have a personal invitation." Dalton tossed the words over his shoulder and strode toward the revolving door.

Rory stayed right on his heels. He refused to look over his shoulder. Doing so would undermine all the bravado Dalton had just shown. They were almost to the door when a different voice hailed them.

"Excuse me, Mr. Knight, I am issuing you your personal invitation."

Dalton's shoulders tensed but he didn't show it as he slowed to a stop and turned in tandem with Rory. Dalton quirked up one eyebrow. "Did you make an appointment with my secretary?"

"No."

Rory studied the man he'd followed. King didn't look quite so impressive as the reputation which preceded him. Shorter than him by at least three inches and Dalton by about six inches put King at just under six feet. His yellowing skin spoke of illness or a really bad fake tan job.

"Why should I give you a second of my time?" Dalton asked casually. "I have everything I need waiting for me at home."

"Ah, but," King pointed to Rory, "your friend doesn't, and I have something he wants."

Shit. Is that confirmation he has Sam?
How the fuck does he know I was the one guarding Adalyn?
Ah, fuck, she's tagged somehow.

He made a mental note to discuss it with Dalton as soon as their asses were clear from here.

"I'm afraid you misunderstand the situation," Dalton replied.

"Come now," King interrupted and approached them. "Shall we talk in my suite where there aren't so many people around to hear our business transactions?"

"You mean where there aren't so many witnesses?" Always one to call a spade a spade, Dalton wasn't going to allow King to gain an inch. Rory knew Dalton well enough to recognize how Nemesis, the warrior, bristled under the mantel of Dalton Knight's, heir to one of the richest oil companies in the world, spoiled attitude.

"That too." King's tone was wry.

You mean it stinks like a hound dog who got close to the rear end of a pissed off skunk?

Yes, yes, I do.

"Why would you think anything you have is important to my friend?"

"Shall we discuss this in my suite?"

"No, I think I prefer to discuss it right here." Dalton shook his head. Every time King had to make the request, it gave Dalton an upper hand. While Rory knew it, it bothered the fuck out of him that Dalton appeared to be forgetting the item King was referring to was a little boy who was probably scared out of his mind. "Tell me what it is you think you possess that I or my friend require?"

Rory saw the annoyance flash in King's eyes before the asshole was able to bank it and whisper the name softly.

"Samuel Cassidy."

It took every ounce of willpower he'd learned over his years in combat to keep his butt in place. He'd sell his soul to someone nefarious to be able to put his fist through the asshole's face right the hell now. But he didn't dare.

"I could kill you both now and nobody would ever talk, and no police would be called." King finally lost his patience.

"You could try it." Dalton shrugged. "Bring it, and see what those red dots on your chest do."

Immediately, two laser dots appeared to hover over King's center mass. The asshole's face paled as he glanced down at them. Rory had to give him some bit of credit that there wasn't a puddle of piss on the floor to go along with the rage on his face.

"I have something you want," King repeated. "You have something I want. Shall we trade?"

"No." Dalton smirked. "You have nothing I want, and everything you want will never be yours."

Jesus, Boss, don't make me kill you. That's Sam you are talking about. Adalyn's son.

"Surely we can come to some agreement."

"Nope." Dalton turned back toward the door. "Knight Oil does not deal with assholes who sell women and children. If that's your game, then our businesses do not cross over and we have nothing further to discuss." Dalton strode to the emergency door next to the revolving one and pushed down on the bar, letting them out onto the street.

"What the fuck, Boss?" Rory whispered as they clattered down the steps.

"Shut it."

"It's Adalyn's son."

"I will not trade my wife and baby for him," Dalton growled. "It's better King gets that fucking idea out of his head right the fuck now."

"You signed his death warrant."

"Hell no." Dalton yanked open the door of an SUV and climbed into it. Rory had no choice but to follow him, as trying to walk from here would only lead King straight back to Adalyn.

"Seriously—"

"Shut it." Dalton pulled his cell phone out of his pocket and slapped it into a holder. "Did you get all that?"

"Son, what the heck have you gotten yourself into?"

"Dad!"

"I understood it," the man on the phone replied. "Why didn't you tell me you were in Paris?"

"I need to know where that fucker goes." Dalton didn't answer his father's question.

"Remi will see what he can do," Mr. Knight Senior muttered. "Your mother is going to be furious."

"I'm sorry, Dad, there's a kid in trouble…"

"And I'm too old to be involved in this mess," Knight

Senior said. "I think I preferred when you would call and tell me you were going to be out of touch for a while and we'd know not to watch the news."

"Me too, Dad."

Rory braced his hand on the oh shit bar as Dalton sped down streets and took lefts and rights like he knew where he was going. Rory knew he didn't; their experience with GPS lady earlier was proof enough of that.

"Dad, I gotta go." Dalton hit end on the call before giving his father time to respond.

"Boss, what the hell?"

"I will not let that fucker think Lina and our baby are ever up for trade." Dalton's voice was stone cold with no emotion. "I don't give a fuck if you think that's wrong…"

"I don't think it's wrong, per se." Jeez, he wasn't a total dick. "But Sam is innocent."

"And if my father hadn't been in that exact hotel today, I'd have found another way." Dalton reached for the phone again and hit speed dial one. "Trev, give me fucking directions before I end up in Bruges or somewhere equally more interesting than the streets of Paris."

CHAPTER TWELVE

Adalyn almost jumped out of her skin when someone knocked police style on the door of the apartment. She was already making her way to the door when she remembered that Rory had told her not to open the door until he came back. She stared at the door as it moved under the force of someone's fist again. She opened her mouth to ask who it was, but snapped it shut again. Maybe she shouldn't say anything either.

"Adalyn, it's Jeep," a man's voice called.

Jeep? That was one of Rory's friends.

But not Rory.

"I need to know you are okay," Jeep called.

"Adalyn, pick up the phone." Trev's voice was slightly distorted through the phone. "Adalyn, are you there?"

She went back to where she'd placed the phone on the kitchen counter while she'd been cleaning. "I'm still here."

"One of our men, Jeep, is at the door," Trev said. "Let him in."

"No."

"Excuse me?"

"Rory said to let no one in until he is here," she explained. "I promised…"

"Okay." Trev huffed in annoyance. "I don't have time for this. I'll tell Jeep."

"Thank you." She refused to apologize for sticking to her word. Surely all these men could find at least one brain cell between them to figure it out. If they couldn't then they could ask the woman on the team. She'd hopefully be more reasonable.

"Jeep is watching the door," Trev advised her. "If you need him, either open the door or scream. Got it?"

"Yes."

She placed the phone back on the counter and snapped back on her rubber gloves before sticking her hands into the sink. As much as she wanted to know what was going on, she figured by being unreasonable Trev wouldn't tell her.

If you distract him with questions when he's trying to help Rory catch the King, it wouldn't be a good move, and they may refuse to help you find Sam.

She picked up the sponge and pressed it against the plate, scrubbing as hard as her injuries would allow. If she focused on the pain in her fingertips, then maybe she could keep from screaming.

She'd washed and dried every single dish in the kitchen by the time Trev called her name again.

"Adalyn?"

"Yes?" She pulled off her gloves, wincing when the rubber snapped back onto her fingers.

"Rory is coming up the stairs."

"Thank you." She was grateful Trev, which she was assuming was short for Trevor, had kept the line open for her all this time. Although she was sure it wasn't any fun to be listening to the sounds of her cleaning the kitchen. "When he lets me know he's there, I'll open the door."

"I think I like you," Trev muttered. "You understand security."

"I don't want a repeat of the last few days," she reminded him drily. "Once was quite enough."

"I'll bet."

"Adalyn?" The knock, even though she was expecting it, made her jump. "It's Rory."

She walked to the door and peered through the peephole. "I can't see you past whoever is standing in front of the glass."

"Move, Jeep." Rory's voice filtered through the door, and she could just about make out the distorted shape of Rory.

Adalyn unlatched the door and twisted the deadbolt. While she was sure neither would have kept these men out if they'd really wanted to get in here, she was grateful they'd given her the illusion of safety. She stepped back just in time to avoid being hit on the nose with the door as it opened.

"Hi."

Rory stared at her for a second or two before he swept her into a hug and buried his nose into her hair.

"Um." She awkwardly patted his back, unsure what caused this reaction to seeing her again. Aside from Sam, she wasn't typically a hugger unless she knew someone very well, so standing here with her arms around him, petting his back as the others filed into the room was not only strange for her, but also unnerving. "What happened? Are you okay?"

"Yeah," Rory whispered softly. He brushed a soft kiss against the side of her neck. "Sorry." He straightened and stepped away from her. "I don't know what came over me."

"Hormones," Snow deadpanned. "It's always the hormones."

"Shut up."

Adalyn ignored the bickering. "I have some pasta sauce

cooking." She nodded toward the kitchen. "There wasn't much food to work with. I just need to put on the noodles."

"You didn't need to cook for us." Rory frowned as he scanned the living room. "And why did you clean?"

"Because not cleaning means sneezing," she reminded him. "Been there, done that, and it hurts." He followed her into the kitchen. "Did you find your King?"

"He's not my King." Rory propped his butt against the kitchen counter and watched her fire up the gas burner under the pasta pot. "But yeah, we found him."

"And?"

"Uh…"

"He has your son." Dalton stood in the kitchen doorway, one hand resting up high on the door frame. "He wants my wife and child for your son."

"What?"

"What the hell, Boss?"

"She has to know…"

Rory caught her when she stumbled, preventing her from face-planting into the stove. This could not be happening. It. Could. Not. Be. Happening. "This is some kind of sick joke, right?" She pleaded with Rory to tell her Dalton was just a jerk who got his rocks off by being the jerkiest jerk who ever jerked.

"I'm sorry."

"No." The wail bubbled out of her chest. Rory tugged her back into his arms, turning them away from the others as he rocked back and forth, making shushing noises.

"It will be okay," he promised. "We'll figure it out. We'll get him back." One hand left her back for a second before returning. When the kitchen door slammed behind them, she hoped Rory's boss had left the room. If she looked at him, she might throw up.

"Shh, baby, I promise we will find him." Rory kept

rocking and whispering reassurances. "I swear I won't stop until we do."

"We have to go there right now." She pulled back and turned toward the door. "Where is this King? I'll talk to him myself."

"Nuh-uh." Rory snagged her arm and gently stopped her from storming out of the room. "You will put others in danger."

"He's my son, my baby…"

"I know, Momma Bear. I swear I know." Rory ignored her hands as they swatted at him. He wrapped his arms around her again as she tried to push him away. "I don't know how we're going to do it, but we will do it."

"I need…"

"I know. I know." He wiped the tears from her eyes. "But if King is involved, the last thing we want is him getting his hands on you again."

"He can have me," she retorted. "Me for Sam, each and every time." This could not be happening. How was this happening? "I will find him." She mustered up every ounce of fierceness she could find in her body and pushed it into her voice. "I will find him."

"Yes," Rory agreed. "But make it WE will find him."

She was going straight out the door and going to march right down the street until she found this King person. She no longer cared what the others would think or how hurt she was. Sam was out there, and she wouldn't stop until she got him back. Silently promising herself that nothing was impossible, and good things could happen, she sniffed hard and pulled back just as the pasta pot boiled over. She glanced at the pot, and back to Rory. Bless him, he was trying to help, but even she could see he was very far out of his depth. "Tell your asshole boss to cook his own damn dinner."

"I will." Rory smiled at her.

Good, he was taking her snark as compliance. Awesome, let him think that. He—no, they were all about to learn how deep a mother's love really went. She pulled out of his arm and swept out of the kitchen with her head held high and into the bathroom, slamming the door behind her as hard as she could.

CHAPTER THIRTEEN

Rory winced at the slam of the door, not because it bothered him, but because the movements must have hurt Adalyn. He scowled toward where Dalton was on the phone across the room.

What a dick.

But even as he said the words in his head, he knew they were unfair. It was an impossible situation to be in. Even so, rage bubbled and fought its way up from somewhere deep inside him. He must have blacked out. Maybe rage really did have the red haze you read about in books, as the next thing he knew, he was across the room with his fist slamming into Dalton's jaw. His boss staggered back, the phone in his hand flying across the room.

"Mokaccino, what the hell…?" Jeep jumped over the back of the couch, body checking him as he moved in for another punch.

"I'll give you that one," Dalton snarled. "Try that again and you and me are gonna have problems."

"We already have problems." He spat out the words. "Her child is innocent."

"So. Is. Mine." Rage dripped from each word, and Rory understood it. He did.

"Your child isn't more important than Adalyn's."

"It is to me." Dalton sat heavily on the arm of the couch. "But that doesn't mean I'm stopping looking for him…"

"You fucking practically told King that Sam means nothing to you."

"Because if he thinks he does, do you think there is any way in hell that he'll give him up without getting my Lina or my kid?"

"He might kill him because he is of no use to him." There, he'd said it, the fear of what was to come which terrified him more than anything ever had. Even coming face-to-face with a rattler sleeping in his niece's crib while he'd been babysitting her hadn't caused fear like this. "He's only a little boy."

"And mine hasn't had a chance to take his first breath yet." Dalton's voice caught and hitched. "My kid deserves a chance to live, and my wife a chance to be free. I will not offer up one for the other. Period."

"Understood."

"My father is still at the hotel," Dalton reminded him. "He's going to be having lunch with King, or at least attempt to."

"What fucking good will that do?"

"Because Dad is going to convince King that his daughter-in-law is a gold digger and that he's looking for a way to get her out of my life."

Everyone in the room snorted. "Next time you piss me off, Boss," Jeep deadpanned, "I'm telling Lina you called her a gold digger."

"I want to be there when you do," Logan muttered. "Please tell me when you do that."

"You got it, bro."

A sharp whistle split the air, stopping everything in its

tracks. "Hey, dumbasses," Snow called. "While y'all were measuring dicks and deciding on whose family is more important, Adalyn took off down the fire escape. Get your shit together, stat."

"She wouldn—" But he knew she would; there wasn't a damn thing on the planet Adalyn wouldn't do for her kid, including put herself right into danger. "She doesn't know where King is." He bolted for the door.

"Doesn't seem to matter to her." Logan stayed right on his heels as they took the stairs two at a time.

"Yeah." He pushed out onto the street, this time with a hell of a lot less care than he had earlier, and turned toward the hotel. "Split up." He didn't care that he was giving orders instead of waiting for Dalton or Jeep to do it. "Find her."

He glanced over his shoulder at Jeep and Dalton as they hurried after him. "This is on you," he warned his boss.

"Yeah."

"It sounds like she means more to you than just a principle," Jeep remarked.

Rory didn't bother to dignify that with a response. He didn't understand the hows or whys, and he really didn't care; he could figure those things out later. Adalyn mattered. Sam mattered. End of discussion. "They matter," he confirmed. "They matter a lot."

"Shit," Dalton muttered softly.

First Rory thought he was realizing how much Adalyn and Sam meant to him, but when he spotted her standing at the foot of the steps leading to the hotel, dread and fear sped up his steps. "Fuck." He ruthlessly pushed through a bunch of teenagers, ignoring their cries of outrage, and reached Adalyn. He wrapped one arm around her waist and tugged her with him as he kept moving past the hotel. Lifting her off her feet to do it hadn't been part of the plan, but he wasn't going to change that right now either. "It's me. Rory." He spoke over her screech of alarm. "Please keep coming with me."

"That's where I was." She struggled in his arms. "Sam might be in there."

"We have people in there." He remembered Dalton's father, although he had no clue what an old man could do against King and his fucking snakes. "If you march in there right now you jeopardize everyone, including Sam."

"But—"

He stepped into an alleyway and placed her gently on her feet. "Don't run," he warned as he crowded her up against the wall. "Do you trust me?"

"No—"

His stomach fell.

"Yes—no—I don't know."

Fuck. That isn't exactly a no, but it's not a ringing endorsement either.

"Which is it?" he asked. "Yes or no?"

"I—um—I suppose."

"That will have to do." He was going to ignore the twinge of disappointment from her refusal answer in a way which made sense. "We will get Sam." He repeated his promise from earlier. "I swear we will get him."

"I want to believe you." Her shoulders slumped. But this time he didn't dare trust it was in defeat. Hell no, his girl, she'd take off after her kid again the second an opportunity presented itself.

"But you don't," he whispered. "Believe me, I mean."

"Sam can't afford for me to leave anything to chance."

"I know." He understood it. Hell, he agreed with her. "Over the years we've seen so many parents kicking over stones and moving mountains trying to find their missing children. But you…" He brushed her hair back from her face and tipped her face up so he could look in her eyes. "You have something those parents didn't have."

"What's that?"

"Us."

"Damn straight."

Rory's jaw clenched when he heard Dalton's whispered words behind him, and Adalyn snorted.

"You expect me to believe you will help me?" she spat at Dalton. "After you saying you wouldn't back there?"

"I didn't say I wouldn't help." Dalton stepped up next to him. "I said I wouldn't put my wife and baby on the line to do it. That's a big difference than saying I won't help."

"Whatever."

"My father." Dalton bent down, almost over Rory's shoulder. "Right now, my father is in that hotel, fishing for information," he informed her. "If you think I have any less feelings for my father than I do my wife, then you've lost your damn mind. But I saw an opportunity and took it. Thankfully, my old man is smart enough to play along."

"Is that true?"

"Yes, baby, it's true."

"Shit."

He held out his hand, palm up. "Will you come back to the apartment with me?"

"I think they are called flats over here." She put her hand into his and he closed his fingers over hers. "You won't stop—"

"I swear we will keep looking."

"Okay."

Thank fuck, the last thing he wanted to do was carry her as she struggled against him through the streets. He'd land all their asses in jail for human trafficking. That was one charge which would never apply to Nemesis Inc.

"But we call the police," she added as they turned out of the alleyway and onto the street. "We call the police and make a report the second we get back to the flat."

Fuck!

CHAPTER FOURTEEN

CALLING the police was a reasonable thing to do. Right? On what planet did stuff like what was happening to her happen and the police were not called? This wasn't some TV show where everything was resolved in an hour-long episode. This nightmare was lasting way longer than an hour. She needed it to be over now. Adalyn strained her eyes, peering in at the hotel. Trying to see through the walls, hoping and praying for a glimpse of Sam. Once they were past the steps, she turned her head unwilling to look away until distance forced her to do so.

"We'll find him." Rory caught her as she stumbled over an uneven piece of pavement.

She appreciated how he kept trying to reassure her. She just wasn't sure she believed him. She'd traveled enough to know shitty things happened to good people. "What happens now?" She needed him to say they would call the police. They had to be able to help.

"Trev will put clues together and find your boy." Dalton pushed open the door to the apartment building. "If my dad can find out something, anything, that will make things a hell of a lot easier." He shut the door behind them. "For now, we pack our shit and move. We're too close to King. There's no way he didn't have someone follow us."

"You saw that, huh?" Jeep turned around to scan the street before he shut the door after them.

"I'm pissed off as all get out," Dalton grumbled. "That didn't affect my vision or situational awareness."

"Someone followed us?" She hadn't seen anyone out of the ordinary. Were they trying to scare her more than she already was? "Is this some trick to get me to leave with you?"

"No." Rory positioned her in front of him and behind Dalton as they climbed the stairs. "You weren't meant to see him. We did, as knowing what's happening is how we stay alive."

"I think you are all bullshitting me."

"To what purpose?"

His tone was light, and she had to be imagining the hurt she heard in his voice. What did he have to be hurt over? Her son was missing. M.I.S.S.I.N.G for God's sake. "I—"

"Having someone scouting on the outskirts of the area is pretty standard for these guys," Logan said. "It can be used if you are a bodyguard for someone too, especially if you don't want people to know that person has personal protection. Although it's not as effective as a show of force, or letting the bad guys know they have to get through a bunch of burly guys to get to their target," Logan explained.

"Okay." That made sense to her. She'd used similar tactics in her own writing. And, lord, if anyone in authority got a good look at her Google history, she'd end up on some country's watch list for certain. Probably a lot of countries' watch lists.

"Gather your shit," Dalton ordered. "Five minutes and we're out of here."

"Where are we going?"

"I don't know," Rory replied. "But probably another safe house. If it was just the boss, he'd probably waltz straight back into that hotel and ask for a room."

"Can we do that?" She sat on the couch. She still had nothing but the clothes Snow and Logan had purchased for her. Those were still in the shopping bags where she'd left them next to the front door earlier.

"Hell no." Rory sank onto his haunches in front of her. "When we find Sam, and we will find him." He tucked a lock of hair behind her ear. "He's gonna need you to be in one piece. He'll need your support more than he ever has before."

Adalyn leaned forward, placed her hands on Rory's arms, and leaned her head into his chest. She sighed in relief when he didn't push her away but instead moved her hands from his arms to his waist and wrapped his around her. "I'm so scared," she whispered softly. "I need him to be okay."

"We will find him." He'd repeated the words so much at this point she wasn't sure who he was trying to convince, himself or her. But she needed them repeated until Sam was back in her arms.

"He's just a little boy." She hiccupped.

"I know."

A phone rang deeper into the apartment. She couldn't see past Rory's body but recognized Dalton's voice when the ringing stopped.

"Dad? Good. Did he buy it?"

It was disconcerting to listen to just one side of the conversation, but she figured it would go down like a lead balloon if she asked him to put it on speaker.

"FUCK," Dalton said. "We're on our way. I'll meet you at the hotel in about an hour." There was a slight pause where

Dalton was clearly listening to what his father had to say. "Yeah, understood. And, Dad, thank you. See you soon."

"What did he say?" Rory asked the question for her so she didn't have to.

"Now we go meet my dad at his hotel and we wait while Trev and some other tech gurus are working on it," Dalton answered. "Got everything?"

"That's it?" There had to be more information they could give her. It was frustrating as all get out to be asking questions and receiving answers which weren't answers at all, but riddles and wait. "I'm so sick of waiting."

"Welcome to our world." Rory helped her to her feet. "Come on, we gotta move before King's guys get their shit together and storm the castle."

"Do you think they will?" She was so far out of her depth it wasn't funny.

"It's what we'd do," Rory told her.

"I think I preferred living with my ex-in-laws over having my son missing." That was a sentence she never thought would come out of her mouth. Yet here she was. She slipped her hand into his and ignored the dull ache when he wrapped his around them.

"I know." Once again, Rory placed her in front of him in the middle of the group and they left the flat and shut the door behind them. "Do you think they could be involved?"

"I don't know how they would know this King person." She'd been wracking her brain cells trying to figure out a connection, but each and every time she came up empty. "It doesn't mean there isn't a connection there. It just means if there is, I don't know it."

"Yeah." He opened the door of the SUV for her and waited for her to slide into the rear seat. He leaned in over her and secured the seat belt and paused with his face in front of hers. "We will find him, I promise."

"I know you will do your best."

He studied her face for so long she was sure he didn't believe her, but then he nodded, straightened out of the SUV, and slammed the door. "Ready, Boss." Rory slid in next to her on the back seat and shut the door after him.

"I have The Four X's running interference." Dalton drove out of the parking spot. "If you shoot one of the McKinley brothers, we are fucked."

"Don't shoot your fancy rich boy cousins," Rory muttered. "Got it."

"Dude, I don't claim that lot of hooligans as family," Dalton muttered. He slid their SUV into Paris traffic. "They are the crazy stepchildren we inherited when my aunt married their father. Worst mistake I ever made was bringing Gunnar home with me from Buds," Dalton grumbled. "It opened a whole can of worms that should have stayed shut."

"Does he not like them?" she asked Rory softly. Even though she knew Dalton could probably hear her too, his snort confirmed it.

"Eh, he likes them at Christmas or sometimes at weddings." The corner of Rory's mouth quirked upward. "Never at funerals."

"Does anyone like anyone at funerals?"

"Nope, probably not," Rory agreed. "Funerals are where your presence is required, not requested, and you can guarantee the day is always going to suck."

"Truth." She turned to watch the Paris streets as they flew past the window. Funerals were one thing she didn't want to think of. Nightmares were already in her future; she didn't need to invite more of them in by thinking of funerals and dying.

CHAPTER FIFTEEN

Rory shouldn't have been surprised when Dalton followed the SUV in front of them into one of the swankiest hotels on the outskirts of Paris. Yet every single time evidence of Knight Oil's money became evident he was surprised. It was far from fancy fountains and beautiful gardens filled with roses he'd been reared. He resigned himself to remembering not to touch anything in case he broke it.

"Um, wow." Adalyn whispered the words so softly he almost didn't hear them.

"Right?" He unclipped his seat belt. "Wait there. I'll come around and help you out."

"I'm more than capable of getting out of the car all by myself," she called after him.

He yanked open the door and grinned down at her. "But I like helping you." He offered his hand, and she took it.

"Why?"

"I just do." The woman wrote romance, how the hell did she not understand the nuances that came with an alpha male looking after his woman?

Oh, she's yours, is she?

Shut it.
She could be.
I'd like her to be.

Admitting that to himself was unnerving but he slapped it on his mental list of shit to deal with later and shoved it aside. Adalyn needed him to look after her. To find her son. She didn't need him panting after her like a dog after a bitch in season. No matter how much he wanted to scratch the itch, which was almost driving him to insanity, he wanted to be there for her for more than that.

If she'll let you.
Yeah.
That.
If she'll let me.

He smiled when her hand snuck into his, and he laced their fingers together. "Ready."

"Do you think this fancy schmancy hotel has a bath?"

"I think we can wrangle one of those for you." He lowered his head so he spoke next to her ear. "We may even be able to bribe someone to provide you with bubbles if that's your jam for a bath."

"Sold." She tugged on his hand and hurried ahead. "What are you waiting for, Moka? Let's go."

"Two to a room." Dalton was saying at the check-in desk. "Yes, all under the Knight Oil account." He glanced over his shoulder, scanning the room. "Can you call my father and let him know we have arrived?"

"Of course, Sir." The receptionist scanned her computer and picked up a phone. "I can put you in touch with him right now."

Rory decided he liked this way of doing things. The receptionist didn't give out Knight Senior's room number, and the desk covered their view of the phone, ensuring they couldn't figure it out from the number she'd dialed.

"Mr. Knight, Sir, I have your son and his guests here in the lobby. Would you like to speak with him?" the receptionist spoke into the phone. "Of course, Sir. One moment please." She held out the phone to Dalton. "He'll speak with you now, Sir."

"Thank you." Dalton took the phone and stepped to one side, allowing them all to approach the desk and check in.

"May I have your name please, Sir, Madam?" the receptionist asked.

"John Murphy." Rory gave the name he typically used to check into hotels when they were on jobs. He dug into his pocket for the fake driver's license the receptionist would need to log his name into the system.

"Saffron Cassidy." Clearly Adalyn had picked up on his use of the fake name and decided to use her pen name instead of her real one. He nodded in approval. Good, she was fast on the uptake and smart.

"Mr. Murphy, you are in room four oh one." The receptionist ran a keycard through the machine and laid it on top of the glass counter. "Ms. Cassidy, you are right next door with Ms. Black."

"I prefer a single room," Adalyn replied. "I can pay separately if that's an issue."

"No, that's—"

"Give us a moment please." He didn't like either of those options. He tugged Adalyn to one side and let Logan and Snow next to the counter.

"I can stay in a room by myself," she whispered furiously, not even giving them time to be out of earshot.

"Please stay with me." He put one finger under her chin and tipped her face up. "Or at least share with Snow." He had to make her understand. "We don't know if King knows we are here..." He trailed off, giving her a moment to fill in the blanks. It was fucking adorable how she chewed on her bottom lip as she thought about his request. He was a fucking sap for noticing stuff he'd given the others shit for over the years. He took all the teasing back. He got it now.

"Then I stay with you."

He blew out a breath of relief. "We can ask for two beds."

"Okay, good, and a bath."

"Yes, Ma'am." He led her back to the receptionist's desk and stood behind Logan as he sorted out a room for himself. When his team brother was done checking in, he nodded and stepped back up to the desk. "Ma'am, we need a twin room with a bath for me and Ms. Cassidy."

"Of course, Sir." The receptionist tapped some keys on her computer. "I have a suite on the fourth floor where the other rooms are, but it's more expensive than only a twin with a bath, which is on the fifth floor."

"We'll take the suite," he decided.

"You spending my money to impress your lady friend again, Murphy?" Dalton called.

"Yes, Sir."

"Can I kill him?" Adalyn whispered. "At least let me kick him. That's allowed, right?"

"Not at reception." The receptionist smiled at her. "But if you are in the suite, we have some big French press coffee makers which are ideal for putting men back in line."

"Oh, I like you," Snow jumped in. "Thanks for the tip."

"You're welcome," the receptionist replied. "I'm here to help."

"I can see that." Dalton handed her back the phone. "Are you guys all checked in?"

"I'm just finishing the keycards for Mr. Murphy and Ms. Cassidy." The receptionist placed them on top of the counter. "Do you need me to call for a valet to help with your luggage?"

"No, thank you, Marie," Dalton replied. "They can carry it themselves."

"As you wish," Marie replied. "I hope you enjoy your stay."

"Does it feel like we are living in hotels nonstop?" Adalyn asked him as they waited for the elevator. "Not that I'm complaining about being in such a beautiful place, but it feels all kinds of wrong that I am in the lap of luxury, and I don't know where Sam…"

Rory tugged her in under his arm, offering what comfort he could in public. "I know." He didn't want to upset her by telling her of the possible conditions her son was in. But he also didn't want her to not take advantage of a five-star luxury hotel while they had the chance. This stuff didn't happen very often, and he knew the only reason they were even here now was because Knight Senior was staying here.

It had been faster than he'd expected it to be for them to check in. The slight hiccup when Adalyn realized she'd have to share a room with either him or Snow was easily fixed.

She chose to stay with me.

Don't go reading too much into that.

But no matter how much he reminded himself not to… he kinda did.

Once they hit the fourth floor, he led her down the hallway, checking room numbers as he went. "We're the next one."

"Okay."

They stopped outside the door, and he slid the keycard into the slot. The light flashed green and the door unlocked, allowing them to enter. Even though this was a hotel Dalton and his family clearly trusted, Rory still drew his weapon and silently tucked Adalyn in behind him before entering the room. He smiled when he felt her fingers wrap into his belt at his back. She remembered the process from when they'd entered Caroline's flat earlier today. Had that really been only a few short hours ago? It felt like they'd lived a thousand lifetimes since this morning. "It's clear."

"Wow, it's so beautiful." Adalyn's hand slipped free of his belt, and he watched her turn in a circle taking in the living room. The suite had two bedrooms, a small kitchenette, and one massive bathroom with a jacuzzi tub.

"This is how the other half lives." He snorted. "We don't live like this every day of the week."

"Yeah, me either."

He lowered his go bag to the floor and took the shopping bag holding her clothes from her. "How about I run you that bath?"

"I can fill it."

"No." He went to the bedside table and picked up a folder. "You can pick what you want from room service while I get the bath going. I'll order the food just before you tell me you are ready to get out."

"Oh my god, did we turn off the stove in the flat?"

"Yeah, the guys took care of it," he called over his shoulder. "Jeep took out the trash too."

"Oh, good. I had visions of it burning to the ground because I was distracted and while I can afford to pay for a hotel room, there is no way I can pay for damages to a whole apartment."

He reached for one of the white bottles on the shelf next to the tub, unscrewed the top, and sniffed it. His eyes immediately watered from the strong flowery smell. "Whoa, that's strong."

"You aren't meant to put it right under your nose and inhale it." Her soft laughter wrapped around him. "I promise it's probably not that strong when you run it under the faucet."

"If you say so." He shrugged and did as she suggested. What the hell did he know about bubble baths? Absolutely nothing, that was what he knew about bubble baths. "Did you decide what you'd like to eat?"

"Grilled cheese and soup please." She came into the bathroom and sat on the closed lid of the toilet. "I'll probably want to sleep the second I get out of the tub."

"Yeah. It's been a long few days for you. Don't be so hard on yourself, okay?"

"Yeah."

"Okay, the water is almost over the openings." He got to his feet. "You should be okay to get in soon."

"Rory?"

"Yes?"

"Thank you for looking after me. I don't know that I have the energy to do it all myself."

"There's nothing wrong with that," he told her. "Sometimes even the strongest of us need an extra hand or two at times."

"I know, but I still appreciate it."

"Do you need help getting undressed?"

"Classy, Rory, Classy." There it was, her snark. "I bet you say that to all the girls."

"Nope." He grinned at her. "Just the ones I run a jacuzzi for."

"Sweet talker."

"Shout at me if you need me, okay?" He knew that sounded cheesy as fuck, but he didn't care. "Please don't try to be a hero and do it all yourself if you aren't able."

"I'll be fine, I promise. Shoo."

"I'm going. I'm going." He held both hands up with his palms toward her as he backed out of the bathroom. "Don't lock the door, please. If I have to break it down, Dalton will be pissy."

"Ugh, let's not have that happen." She shuddered. "I don't think I'm in the mood for that again." Her fingers worked at the buttons on her shirt. "Go on, I'll be okay. I promise."

As much as his eyes wanted to stay lasered in on the work her fingers were doing, he nodded and tugged the door shut behind him.

CHAPTER SIXTEEN

ADALYN JERKED AWAKE, sitting straight up in bed. The bath and the food had made her feel more like herself than she had in days. She'd been way overconfident in her abilities and had insisted on sleeping by herself. The joke was on her as the nightmares had been waiting for her as soon as her eyes had closed. "Is that singing?" She cocked her head to one side and listened. "Is the TV on?"

She climbed off the bed and scowled at the covers she hadn't bothered to get under. Even with the air conditioning running at almost full blast she'd decided it was too hot for sheets and blankets. She glanced down at her clothes and adjusted her tank top. "Good thing you checked," she told herself in the mirror before she padded out of the room and into the living room. "Where is that noise coming from?" She peered at Rory's closed door and padded across the living room to press her ear against it.

Hearing nothing, she turned toward the bathroom and listened for the humming noise she'd heard. She didn't think it had woken her up. She had the nightmare to thank for that.

The closer she got to the bathroom door, the louder the humming got. "Rory?" she called softly. "Are you in here?"

"Mm, mm, mm."

She pushed open the door and peered in, her eyes widening at the sight which greeted her. Rory lay in the tub, surrounded by bubbles. A yellow duckie floated down near his toes. She could just about make out the headphones in his ears as he hummed and sang softly along with Bruce Springsteen's "I'm on Fire".

"Oh."

"Hi, baby." Rory rolled his head on the rim of the tub to look at her. "Are you okay?"

"Um…" He expected her to talk when he straightened in the bath like that and she had a good view of his chest? The bubbles clung to the hairs, and she scanned down his stomach to the water line which hid important bits of him. "You're naked."

"Hah." He snorted. "I usually get naked when I jump in the tub." He nudged the duckie with his knee, putting it within hands reach. "Did you meet Charles?"

"Charles?" She spun around, scanning the living room, tugging down the bottom of her T-shirt to cover her butt. Her sleep shorts were way too short to have someone else in the suite.

"Charles." Rory grabbed the duckie and waved it before zooming him around the water, making truck and then duck noises.

"You've lost your mind." That had to be it. "Or did you drink?"

"Just water." Rory paused Charles's lap of the tub and sent him in the opposite direction. "Mmh, at night I wake up with…" he sang softly. "I swear I'm not drunk, or on drugs," he clarified. "I've just learned that there comes a time when my sanity requires me to act like a five-year-old in the tub."

"You have lost your mind." She knew her eyes had to be wide. She could feel her hair line touching her eyelids. The good thing was it didn't hurt. The bad thing she probably looked like a total idiot. "Do I need to call Logan or one of the other guys?"

"Hell no." He dropped the yellow duckie and braced his hands on the edge of the tub. "Please don't punish me like that." He smirked at her. "Cover your eyes unless you want to see something I'm not sure you are quite ready for."

"No, no, don't get out," she implored him. "I'm going to make coffee or tea or something." Stumbling and stuttering over her words, she fled the bathroom with his soft laughter chasing her into the living room. "You're a jerk."

"But I'm a fun one."

It was almost impossible to be annoyed with him when he sounded very much like Sam did when he was up to mischief. She recognized the tone and while her heart ached for her son, it also smiled in happiness for the warrior who could still find joy in playing with a rubber duckie in the jacuzzi.

She searched in the fridge for the bottled water, filled the kettle, and set it to boil. She found the grounds and measured them into the French press. She paused and considered how strong that amount of grounds would make the coffee, before adding an extra half scoop. Rory didn't seem like a man who drank his coffee weak. "He'll just have to deal with coffee where the spoon doesn't stand upright all by itself for once." She poured the water in, stirred it, and let it sit for about five minutes before pushing down the plunger.

A quick glance along the countertop showed her a basket filled with individually wrapped croissants and little pots of butter and jam. While she was more than a little certain that she could order fresh croissants from the kitchen, she really didn't want to deal with people at just after five in the morning. She made short work of opening two croissants and heated them up in the toaster, then applied the butter so it melted while the treats were hot. She tugged the basket closer to her and picked up the jams. "Do you have a favorite jam?" She raised her voice and hopefully he would hear her all the way in the bathroom.

"Yeah, strawberry."

"Eep." She jumped and dropped the tiny jar she held in her hand. It shattered on the tile floor. "Dang it. You could have told me you were there. I didn't hear you."

"Don't move," Rory ordered. "Will I hurt you if I lift you on the counter?"

"I don't think so."

"Good." He leaned across the broken glass, wrapped his hands around her waist, and lifted her up to place her on the counter next to the coffee. "Stay there. I'll clean it."

His hands were big enough that his fingers had almost reached all the way around her waist.

When is the last time either my waist was small enough, or a man's hands were big enough to do that?

She shamelessly watched him as he snagged some kitchen paper from the roll next to the microwave and bent to clean the floor. "I'm sorry. I can do it. I shouldn't have dropped it."

"Stay right there," he ordered. "I've got it, no biggie."

"Okay, thank you."

He tossed the handful of paper towels into the trash can then grabbed a broom and swept the floor. "My momma taught me and my brothers how to clean just as much as she did my sisters," he told her. "She said we weren't to be useless lumps around the house and better know how to do shit as once she married us off, she didn't want to deal with a return to sender situation."

"Your momma sounds wise." She couldn't help but want to know more, so she spat out the burning question before she could change her mind or talk herself out of it. "Did she marry you off?"

"Nah, this job doesn't really leave much room for a family."

She should have done that internal fist bump at that little nugget of information. He was single, and that made her ridiculously happy. She narrowed her eyes at him in confusion though. "At least three of your team have families, or at least wives."

"Four. You haven't met Lucifer yet. He's married to a man who works down in Italy."

Well, wasn't that a surprise? She hadn't been expecting that. "He's married to a man, huh?"

"Is that a problem?"

"Not for me." She reached for two mugs while staying on the countertop. "I'm just surprised it is for all of you guys. I've always heard Special Forces are weird about it."

"Luc is a brother. He's a dumbass and gets himself into stupid shit all the time, but we love him."

Crap, she hadn't meant to piss him off. "I swear I'm just curious. I don't mean anything bad by it."

"It's okay." Rory emptied the dustpan into the trash can. "They've had some shit over the years. I guess I'm just a little protective of him and Rome."

"I love that you are."

"Really?" He took the mug of coffee she offered him and dumped two lumps of sugar into it before taking a sip.

"Yes." It was freaking adorable, but she was going to guess that wasn't something he associated with himself very much. "Can we sit on the balcony and watch the sun come up?"

"I don't know if that's a good idea." He leaned against the counter next to her legs and sipped on his coffee.

"Why?"

"Because a balcony is open, and any sniper with a decent aim could take advantage."

"Wow. Way to dampen the mood."

"Yeah." He drank from the cup and lowered it again. "I know you can't stay locked away forever. But while we're here in Paris, I'd kinda like you in one piece."

"You do, huh?" She peered at him over the rim of her cup. "I'd kind of like that too."

They grinned at each other. The easy camaraderie between them wasn't something she was used to. Here, next to this time, during one of the most stressful times of her life, she'd finally found something... nope, not something... someone who felt like home.

That's a problem.

A big problem.

He's not mine.

I'm not his.

I don't know that we can ever be that to each other.

CHAPTER SEVENTEEN

Rory took the croissant Adalyn offered him and took a massive bite. "Thank you." He spoke around the mouthful. "I like that they give us snacks."

"You can never have too many snacks." She pinched the skin of her stomach through her T-shirt. "As you can see, I'm not adverse to snacks."

"Stop it." It irritated him when women thought they had to be skin and bones to be beautiful. "Don't put yourself down like that. Just like a sports car is built for switchbacks, women's bodies are built for curves. There isn't a man I know who doesn't love curves."

"I—"

"Nope." He shook his head. "My sisters are the same and it makes me nuts. If everyone was a—" A knock at the door stopped the rant he'd given at home more times than he could count. "Stay here." He left the kitchen area and snagged his handgun from where he'd placed it on the table near the TV. He double-checked the safety and went to the door to peer out the peephole, lowering his weapon and opening it. "What's doing, Sensei?"

"Eedana for Adalyn." Logan waved his phone. "She's insisting on talking to her."

"Why? Does she think I've corrupted her?"

"Have you?" Logan scowled at his towel.

"Nope, I was in the tub."

"With Charles."

Oh, hell no, she didn't say that out loud in front of Logan.

"Who the fuck is Charles?"

Don't say it. Don't say it. Please don't fucking say it.

"His rubber duckie."

Oh, jeez, I'm gonna kill her. It would be justified.

"His what now?" Logan put the phone to his ear. "Hey, babe, did you hear that? Mokaccino has a rubber duckie called Charles for the tub. Make sure you tell Lina and Willow in front of the guys at dinner tonight."

"Fucker. You're an asshole." He reached for the phone, but Logan was too fast and he threw his arm out, handing the phone off to Adalyn.

"Eedana says it's too late as they've already had dinner."

Thank fuck for small mercies and a reprieve he hadn't expected to get. His stomach dropped when Adalyn grinned at him and he held his breath.

"She'll do it at breakfast instead." Adalyn smirked at him. It was impossible to be mad when she was giggling and smiling more than he'd seen in days. She smiled at him and went back to chatting to her friend on the phone.

Damn it, he could take one for the team. If he didn't make a fuss, maybe they'd forget all about it. But he already knew that was probably wishful thinking.

"How is she doing?"

"She has good moments and bad." He went into his bedroom and grabbed a pair of jeans out of his go bag and pulled them on. "I see the glimpses of the woman she is. But then the momma who's traumatized over her missing kid takes over until she pushes it back behind the mask she wears."

"You noticed that too, huh?"

"Yeah." He hadn't been going to mention it, but it was too late now. "She's working hard to keep it in place. But I can see the fear in her eyes when she thinks I'm not looking."

"Keep doing what you're doing," Logan advised. "From what Dana told me, I'd expected her to be a damn mess on the floor. That she's not tells me she might break at some point."

"Logan, how do I open my Facebook page on your phone?" Adalyn called from the kitchen. "Even the link Eedana is sending me doesn't work."

"I don't have social media on my phone." Logan went to the door. "None of us do."

"Why?" Rory narrowed his eyes at the tightness around her mouth. "What happened?" He reached for his cell. "I can call Trev to give me access, and we can toss this phone afterward."

"Can you do that?"

"Sure." He hit the button to call Trev. Even with the time difference, he knew their comms tech would still probably be at his desk. The man appeared to have no life outside of Nemesis. "Hey, Trev, can you give me access to Facebook?"

"Why on earth would you want to open the book of faces? Don't you know that's just asking for Prince Nakkim from bumfuck nowhere to want to either give you his inheritance or to steal your profile pictures to con some poor woman into thinking the military doesn't pay for us to go home on leave."

"Yeah, those are valid reasons, but Adalyn needs to look at something."

"Her kid?"

He could hear the wheels on Trev's chair squeaking as he

rolled across the floor. "Umm. I don't know. She said she wanted to look on her Facebook page."

"She doesn't have a personal page, so I'm guessing she means her author one. Lemme look."

The tapping of the keyboard told him as usual, Trev wasn't waiting for permission. He was doing it anyway.

"Fuck."

"What?"

"Yeah, she needs to see this, but I don't know how she's going to react," Trev muttered.

"Bad?"

"Yeah, I'm giving you access," Trev said. "Call me back if you need me to scrub that page or if you want me to let loose on some of those keyboard warriors. This is why I don't do social media. Gah."

"Thanks, bro." Rory exchanged glances with Logan. Both of them knew from Trev's reaction they weren't going to like what they found. Rory tapped into the app store and downloaded the program. "Do you have an account? Because I don't."

"Nope, but I know Eedana's login." Logan made gimme fingers, then plucked the phone out of his hand. "Don't look; if I show you her password, both she and Trev will be pissy. And while I quite enjoy pissing off Trev, I have zero inclination to piss off my woman."

"I hear ya, man." He stuck his head around the door of his bedroom and glanced into the kitchen where Adalyn was still talking to Eedana on Logan's phone.

"Here."

Rory snagged the phone from Logan and tapped in Adalyn's author name, then tapped on her profile picture and scanned down the posts on her page.

RORY

I'll never read her again

Didn't even have the decency to say she wasn't coming to Paris. I traveled all the way from Berlin, and she didn't even show up.

Why are authors jerks?

Burning all my Saffron R. Cassidy paperbacks. Who's with me? #entitledauthorssuck.

I hate people. If life happens, fine. But we deserve to know.

I hope she meets the underside of a bus.

"What the actual fuck?" Every single one of those posts reenforced to him why the hell he stayed off social media. How fucking dare they treat her like this? Fine, they didn't know what had happened to her and Sam, but where the hell was human decency? Not one single post asked if she was okay or if anyone had heard from her.

We apologize to all the attendees who attended the signing for Saffron R. Cassidy. We, too, had no indication she wasn't going to show up and are just as devastated as you all are. We are in communication with all other major signings and informing them of her unreliability. Rest

assured we will do everything in our power to ensure she doesn't get to do this to any more readers.

FUCKING ASSHOLES. "Logan, ask Trev to check if there were any missed calls or voice messages on her cell."

"I'll have to wait until she's done talking to Dana." Logan nodded to Adalyn. "She's using my phone."

As if she felt his scrutiny, she looked over that them. "Did you get it open?"

"Yeah." He was so damn tempted to lie to her. He wanted to tell Trev to scrub that page, but he didn't dare lie either. "Logan logged in on Eedana's account."

"Let me see." She jumped down off the countertop. "Dana, I'm giving the phone back to Logan. I've got to deal with this or my career is in the toilet." She paused in front of them. "No, you had to tell me. I needed to know. It's not your fault, sister. I swear. I'll talk to you later. Love you." She handed the phone to Logan. "Dana is convinced that this happened because of my connection to her." She narrowed her eyes at him. "Convince her she's wrong, got it?"

"Yes, Ma'am."

While it was admirable that she didn't want Eedana to blame herself for it, Logan's woman might be onto something in the why all of this was happening. He didn't dare say that though. He handed her the phone and steered her toward the bed. "Sit down, okay?"

"I can't." The words were monotone. "I—oh my God, they hate me."

"It's not your fault."

"I didn't show up." She paced back and forth, scrolling through the phone. "I need to call the organizers and explain…"

RORY

He stepped in front of her, stopping her pacing, and cupped her face with his hands. Even though the bruises were starting to fade to yellow, he was still careful not to hurt her. "Are you sure you are ready for that? There will probably be questions you might not be able to answer."

"I—I have to." He didn't think she was aware she was rubbing her cheek against his palm as if seeking comfort. "This is my business. I won't let that jerk King ruin it too."

"Okay." He wrapped her into a gentle hug. "Hug me for a second, take all the time you need, and when you're ready, log into your own account."

She sighed and laid her cheek against his chest, wrapping her free hand around his waist. "You must think I'm a big baby."

"You aren't a big baby; you survived—"

"But Sam…"

He knew what she'd stopped herself from saying. "We'll get him back." At this point he'd repeated it so many times he was starting to believe himself. Even though he knew better than to make promises he couldn't guarantee, with her he couldn't seem to help himself. He rubbed his chin lightly on the top of her head, giving her all the time she needed. "Maybe we should talk to Dalton first and see what he wants us to say."

"But they are right." She lifted one shoulder. "As far as they know, I just didn't show up."

Rory could tell by her voice that there was no changing her mind. He moved his hands behind her back to get Logan's attention and signed.

Tell the boss.

Logan nodded. Still speaking to Eedana, he made his way to the door of the suite and left.

Adalyn huffed out a breath and pulled back. "I'm ready."

"I'm not leaving," he promised. "I'll be right here next to you if you need me."

"Thanks." She logged out of Eedana's account and into hers. "Crap. I have over three hundred messages…"

"Don't open them." He could already guess what most of them would say. "Just scroll until you find one from the organizer. Or tell me the name and I'll do it for you and hit call, then give you back the phone."

"Ple—please do that."

Tears–holy fuckballs—her tears made his knees want to buckle. It took effort to lock them, so he stayed vertical. The first line of every message he scrolled past made him want to either throw the phone at the wall or puke, or maybe both.

"What's the name, baby?"

"Blue Baton Books."

Can I take a blue baton to their fucking heads?

But he didn't dare say it out loud. She was already upset. He didn't need to make it worse for her. "This one?" He covered the rest of the screen as much as he could with his hand as he showed it to her.

"Yeah." She nodded.

He clicked into the message box and scowled when the latest one came up. "There's no box. Can they block you on this?"

"Yes. Am I blocked?" She tilted the phone toward her, and her face fell when she saw it. "I'm blocked."

"Give me a minute." Rory backed out of the app and called HQ. "Trev, can you get me a phone number for the organizers of Blue Baton Books?"

"Sure thing. Gimme five. I'll send it to your phone."

"Thanks."

"Give me the phone. I'll read the other messages while I'm waiting."

"No way." He wasn't trying to be a dick, but he kinda felt

like one when he looked at the tears in her eyes. "You don't need to read that shit. People will change their tone when you put out a statement."

"You say that like I have a press company. I don't. I'm just a small-time indie author trying to make enough to live simply with my kid."

"I know. I know." He glanced at the door when someone pounded on it. "That's probably the boss," he said over his shoulder as he went to answer it.

"What..." she started to ask. "Logan?"

"Yup." He waved Dalton into the room.

"Big mouth."

Good; if she was throwing shade at Logan then maybe this wouldn't be so bad after all. He glanced at his phone when it buzzed in his hand. "Adalyn needs to call someone," he explained to Dalton. "I figured it might be better if you are here."

"Agree." Dalton pulled the chair which was next to the writing desk toward him and straddled it backward. "Trev filled me in, so make your call when you are ready."

"Why are you being nice?" Adalyn narrowed her eyes at him in suspicion. "You've been like a bear since I met you."

"His wife told him off." Logan grinned. "She's down at the stable with Eedana," he explained.

"Oh." Adalyn's cheeks reddened and Rory was going to guess that she'd been complaining to Eedana about how mean Dalton had been. She'd probably asked for her opinion on how to handle it too. Lina being Lina would have smacked her man upside the head, virtually, as she wasn't close enough to do it in person, and told him to quit being a dick.

"Lina smacked you, huh?" he asked Dalton.

"Pretty much. Doesn't change facts though," Dalton clarified. "But apparently my delivery needs work. I'm sorry I was a dick to you."

"I understand why. Apology accepted."

Could she be any more gracious? He'd been tempted to punch Dalton at least four more times than he'd actually punched him. But maybe it was better not to remind Dalton of that fact or he'd tell Lina, and well, Rory had decided long ago that he was kind of afraid of the boss's wife. "You ready to make that call?" he asked Adalyn.

CHAPTER EIGHTEEN

"No." It was a phone call. It shouldn't scare the crap out of her. But it did. She knew this phone call to the event organizers could make or break Saffron R. Cassidy's writing career. "What do I tell them?"

"Maybe that you had a family emergency," Logan advised. "Surely people understand a family emergency."

"I don't think that's going to cut it." She could see where he was coming from. But they didn't deal with social media on a daily basis. Readers loved to have access to their authors and the vast majority were awesome. "I didn't show up for an event where I was the headline signing author and I didn't let them know I wasn't coming."

"Tell them the truth," Dalton said. "I want to know if they had anything to do with it."

"You think Blue Baton had something to do with me and Sam being kidnapped? Are you insane?"

"Nope." Dalton popped the word. "Both my mom, the Navy, and my wife had me tested. I was clear for insanity."

"I think I preferred him grumpy rather than trying to crack jokes," she muttered out of the corner of her mouth.

She had been hoping only Rory would hear her, but given how Dalton smirked in response, she'd failed, and he heard her anyway.

"I don't know if they had something to do with it or not," Dalton said. "But they knew you were coming here…"

"The whole of romancelandia knew I was coming to this signing."

"What the fu—heck—is romancelandia when it's at home?"

How did she explain it to a man who probably hadn't read a book in years? "It's what the world of romance readers and writers is called. But if you don't read, you probably wouldn't understand."

"Excuse you, I do read, and my wife reads romances, thank you very much," Dalton grumbled. "I didn't know you all had a name for your club thingy." He nodded to the phone. "But call them and let's see what they have to say."

"Okay." She blew out a slow breath. "This is the number, right?" She showed Rory the phone. She knew she was stalling, but she had absolutely no idea what to say. Normally, when she screwed something up, she had to hide away and process it before she could even make an attempt to talk about it. That wasn't an option at this time.

"Yup," Rory confirmed. "Just click into that message, highlight the number, and hit call."

She did as he said and held her breath when the phone started to ring.

"Put it on speaker, please," Dalton said. While it sounded like a suggestion, she took it for the order it was and pressed the relevant button.

"Hello, this is Kristin."

"Kristin, this is Saffron Cassidy."

"You bitch. Who the hell do you think you are…"

"Whoa, enough," Rory interrupted. "If you can't be civil

and refrain from calling Saff names, then I'm ending this call right now. Our family is going through hell, and you don't get to be nasty to her."

"Who the hell are you?"

"That's none of your business, lady." All the while he was talking to Kristin, both his and Dalton's hands were moving. She was guessing this was some kind of sign language as Logan nodded along as if he agreed, although he seemed to be more interested in playing with his phone.

Oh, no, how in the name of words had the call disintegrated into chaos so fast? "Please." She laid her hand on Rory's arm. "Let me talk. It's okay, I promise."

"No, babe, it's not," Rory replied. "She can be civil or have the cops on her front door as a suspect in our kid's kidnapping."

She couldn't have stopped the distressed sound which came out of her soul if she'd tried. There was no way it could have been contained.

"Excuse me? Excuse me?" Kristin tried to get their attention.

"It's her." Eedana's voice was so soft Adalyn almost didn't hear her. She glanced at Logan and frowned. He lifted one shoulder and waved a second phone. She hadn't even heard it ring.

"Who's her?" She was so confused. This was meant to be a phone call to an event organizer to apologize for missing the signing. Not for everyone to be talking in riddles. She pressed end on the call. Kristin didn't need to hear all of this, and handed it to Rory. "Stop it, tell me what's going on?"

"That woman you were speaking to is Kristin Warriner." Logan glanced at Rory and waited for his nod. He'd better not be asking for permission to tell her what the hell was going on. "When Eedana found all the posts on your page, she already knew you were safe. But then she got majorly pissed off at one of the really horrible posts and clicked into the poster's profile to put her on blast for being an asshole…" Logan trailed off.

"Tell me."

"That's when she saw the photo of her at the signing you missed. Photos of her and Kristin."

Understanding dawned. Her friend was crazy if she thought she was going to blame her. "That's why she kept telling me it was her fault?"

Logan nodded.

"How exactly was she meant to know that her former roommate is crazy?"

"I asked her the same thing." Logan scrubbed his hand down his face. "But you know my Dana."

"Yes, yes, I do." She turned first to Rory and then to Dalton. "So the signing was a setup?"

"Our best guess is when the Organization failed to get Eedana to do their bidding, they decided to destroy the only people who matter to her," Dalton said. "They can't get to Logan. But you and Sam…"

"We were vulnerable."

"Yeah. If we had known, I'd have sent an operative here to protect you and Sam."

"I appreciate that, thank you." She did appreciate it, and she understood it wasn't Nemesis Inc.'s fault either. But she couldn't help the regret which welled up inside her. Rory placed a hand on the small of her back, offering comfort and reassurance that he was still there. She shamelessly soaked it in. She didn't want to do this alone. She wasn't even sure how she would deal with it, with help… she just knew that alone, she had no chance at all.

Be logical.

Think.

You can't be the only other person Eedana loves.

Her family are all kinds of whacked....

Oh, crap.

"What about the ladies from her art class?"

"I've sent a team to keep an eye on them," Dalton said.

"And my son?"

"I'm assuming Trev is tracking Kristin's cell phone." Rory glanced at Dalton for confirmation. "And now we know for sure which one she's using. He'll check to see which locations it's pinged off since you and Sam were taken. We know she was here in Paris until at least after the signing."

"Correct," Dalton replied. "My father also confirmed she was present in the hotel with King yesterday."

"He's still in Paris?"

"I don't know that for sure," Dalton said. "Dad didn't see any sign of him there earlier…"

The hope which had started building died again with those words. "Oh."

"I'm sorry." Rory wrapped his arm around her and tugged her into his side. "I wish we…"

"If wishes were horses, beggars could ride." She scrunched her nose up.

"What?"

"Excuse me?"

"You are scrunching your nose." Rory tapped it with his index finger. "You only do that when you are trying to figure something out."

How had he figured that out? But she didn't have time for that.

"What's bugging you?" Rory spun her in his arms to face him. "Tell me."

"Give me a second. I need to work it out in my head." She mentally went through the last few months. "I got invited to this signing almost four months ago," she said slowly. "They said they'd had some cancellations, and I agreed to go." She glanced at Logan. "That was just after Eedana moved in with you, right?"

"Yes."

"So was the signing, the whole thing, a ploy?"

"No. The signing was real," Dalton said. "From what we can figure out, the person who was running it before ran off with all the table signing cash. Is that what it's called? Table signing?"

"Or signup fee. Either one works."

"Well, the last organizer took off with the signup money. A lot of authors were going to be out, flights, hotels, extra books they'd ordered, and a whole host of other shit I don't understand."

"And Kristin swooped in to take over?"

"Yes."

"Bitch."

"I don't think you'll find anyone of us disagree with you there." Rory hugged her tighter.

She didn't even care that his arms were pinching one of the bruises on her ribs. "Those are my readers. My fans. My people. She manipulated all of them to get to me. To get to my son."

"Yeah."

She pinned each one of them in turn with a determined stare. If they wouldn't help her, she'd find another way. "Find that scorpy bitch and make her pay. Promise. Me. You. Will. Make. Her. Pay."

"I swear it," Rory replied immediately.

"What's scorpy when it's at home?" Dalton asked.

"I've only heard it used when Dana sees a scorpion. Is that what you mean? That she's a scorpion bitch?"

"Damn straight."

CHAPTER NINETEEN

Rory released a slow relieved breath. He was an idiot. Someone should take out a full-page advertisement on the front page of the *Washington Post* or something and announce his idiocy to the whole world. He'd been so concerned that this information was too much for her on top of all she was already dealing with, that he'd forgotten how strong Adalyn was. If anything, she no longer sounded devastated. Now she sounded full-on pissed off. It was glorious. She was glorious.

"You got it. I promise we will make her pay."

"Nail her ass to the wall."

"Nope." He shook his head. People could call him a fifteen-year-old boy, but the only ass he was nailing was not going to be Kristin Fucking Warriner's. Just as soon as they'd found Sam and he was sure Adalyn was feeling better, she was his. Nobody called to him or spoke to him quite like she did.

"What do you mean nope?" She pulled out of his arms, put both closed fists on her hips, and glared at him. "You just said you would make her pay."

"I am not nailing her ass to anything." His eyes widened

when both Dalton and Logan snorted with laughter. They got it.

Three.

Two.

One.

He waited what he'd meant to hit her. She wrote romance novels… surely, she could pick up on innuendo with the best of them… apparently she couldn't as the harder his asshole boss and team brother laughed, the angrier she became. "I mean…"

"Go ahead, bro, explain it to her."

"Fuck off, Sensei." Murder was allowed. Even his momma wouldn't object in this instance. Although she'd probably wash his mouth out with soap if she heard his explanation.

"Come on, Sensei, let's go before we get ourselves in shit and I have to pay for another hotel room after you two get into it and forget you aren't sparring on the mats at home." Dalton fisted his hand into Logan's shirt and dragged him out of the room.

"If you aren't going to make her pay, then what are you going to do?"

"Babe…"

"I didn't tell you that you could call me that."

"I like how it fits you coming out of my mouth."

"The only thing that's going to fit in your mouth in a minute is going to be my knuckles as they send your teeth down your throat if you don't start explaining fast."

Damn, she's sexy when she's mad.

He opened his mouth to tell her and snapped it shut again as the sense of self-preservation he'd honed growing up with a bunch of sisters snapped to attention and warned him now was not the time nor the place to be a smartass. He decided to give it to her straight.

Fool, the self-preservation in his head warned.

Don't do it.
Find a better way.

There wasn't a better way, damn it. Better ways required thinking, and even he had to admit that there were times when he wasn't awesome at thinking things through. Put him on a mountainside in a country ending in 'Stan, and he could find you a goat track to get your ass the hell out of there. This situation was not a country ending with 'Stan, and all he had to give her as an escape route was the truth. "I will make her pay. But I'm not nailing her ass… her ass isn't the ass I'm interested in." He saw exactly when the penny dropped as she reddened from the top of her tank top, up her neck. Her cheeks darkened and her eyes widened.

"Wha—at?"

He winced when she screeched the word. Maybe telling her the truth hadn't been a good idea. He tramped down the disappointment. He'd thought they had been building a connection, something to move forward from. He'd been wrong. All he could do now was brazen it out. "I'm not going to tell you I will nail some other chick when the only one I am interested in is standing right in front of me." He stepped toward her… she was worth the risk of that punch she'd threatened him with. "She's mad as hell. Sexy as fuck. And pushing every single one of my buttons. Every. Single. One."

"Have you lost your mind?"

"No." He shook his head. "But I know you aren't ready, and I know that you can't think of anything but Sam and fixing things with your work right now." It was only fair to warn her after all. "But once I find Sam." He held up his hand silently, asking her to let him finish. When she huffed in annoyance but still nodded, he continued, "And I will find him for you. All I'm asking for is a chance to see if this thing sparking between us is something we want to—I don't know—pursue—try?"

"Why are you telling me this?"

"Because there is no way in hell I want you thinking you are in this on your own any longer." He jabbed his thumb into his chest. "I am in this with you all the way until you tell me to leave."

"Oh."

Crap; she could blank her face better than most warriors he knew. What did 'oh' mean? Was that 'oh yes?' or maybe 'oh hell, no?' He ran his hand over his head from front to back in frustration his inability to read this woman caused him. "Oh?"

"Yes, oh."

"Um." He shifted from one foot to the other. "What does 'oh' mean, exactly?"

"I means I don't know what to say."

"It's not a no. I'll take it."

"No." It was her turn to look unsure of herself. "But I'm warning you now that Sam will be my priority…"

"I agree, a billion percent." It was enough. It had to be enough, and her son would always come first. He had to. "I promise I'll put him first too."

"Okay. I'm going to go shower."

"Hey." He walked after her. "Wait."

"Yes?"

He stopped in front of her and cupped her cheek. This time, instead of tilting her head up, he lowered his to press a kiss to her forehead and closed his eyes at the feel of her breath on his throat. "Thank you."

"Why are you thanking me?"

"Because you didn't knee me in the balls or tell me to fuck off." He grinned down at her. "I was aware that might be a possibility." He kissed her forehead again. "Go on. Go have your shower, and I'll see if I can find us something decent for breakfast."

"'kay."

He watched her until she disappeared into the bathroom. "Jeez, I hope I didn't just fuck everything up."

"You didn't," she called through the bathroom door. "I just need Sam back… before…"

"I get it, babe. I promise." Fuck, he hoped he could give her that. Not for himself. But for her, and for Sam.

"Good."

"Breakfast." Muttering to himself, he strode back into the living room. Now that he'd put her on advance notice of his intentions, he wasn't sure if he felt better or worse, maybe a mix of both. Better because she knew right down deep to her bones that he was in her corner, and worse because it was going be at least six of the seven realms of hell to keep his hands to himself until she asked for more. "You're an idiot, Costa, a bona fide idiot."

―――

"Thank you, Sir." The bellhop who'd delivered their breakfast smiled in thanks. "Enjoy your breakfast." He pulled the door shut behind him.

Rory double-checked the locks and wheeled the cart further into the room. He was sure the hotel thought he was insane when he'd requested that they either fold the tablecloth instead of draping it over the cart or leave it off altogether. But he wasn't risking having someone hiding in the cart. He'd seen way too many of those B-grade movies, thank you. He lifted each of the lids, checking the contents and closing them again. "Ada, babe, breakfast." He moved all the plates from the cart and placed them on the coffee table next to the couch.

"Hi." She appeared in the bathroom doorway, wrapped in

a bathrobe with the hotel's initials monogrammed on the pocket. "That smells yummy."

"Come and get it." He waited for her to pick which side of the couch she wanted. "I hope you don't mind eating on the couch."

"Not at all; a couch is always more comfy than a chair any day of the week."

"My momma would have swatted my head if I said that." He sat next to her and carefully pulled the table closer.

"It's a good thing your momma isn't here then."

"Yeah. It is." He lifted the lids off the plates. "I hope you like bacon and pancakes."

"Bacon fixes everything." She smiled at him, then nudged him with her elbow. "Shall we eat before it goes cold?"

"Yes." He handed her a set of cutlery and picked up the remote. "I'll find us something to watch on the box."

"Not the news." She crunched on a piece of bacon. "Anything but the news."

"Deal. Cartoons it is."

"You are a big kid behind it all."

"Yup." He grinned at her, then nodded to her plate. As comfortable as he was right here right now, his gut told him something was coming. He knew better than to ignore that feeling. He shook it off, not wanting her to pick up on his unease. "Eat before it goes cold."

"I'm eating, I'm eating."

CHAPTER TWENTY

When she couldn't fit another bite into her stomach, Adalyn patted it and sighed in contentment. "I'm stuffed. I can't fit another bite."

"Mind if I...?" Rory gestured to the remaining pancake and bacon on her plate.

"Knock yourself out." She curled her feet under her and leaned against his shoulder. What he'd said to her earlier should have sent her running for the hills, screaming for Dalton to assign someone else to look after her. But it didn't. She watched the cartoons on the TV without actually seeing what the cat and the mouse were doing, using it as something to focus on rather than following their antics. When his phone buzzed on the table with an incoming text message, she knew. She just knew. "Sam?"

Rory scanned the message. "Yeah, get dressed. We gotta go."

"What does it say?"

He handed her the phone, pushed the table back to make room to stand, and got to his feet. She read the message.

. . .

Text: **TG LOC. Nem452. stat, WU 60.**
Text: **Copy.**

"This is gibberish." She jumped off the couch and followed him to his bedroom door. "I don't understand what it means."

"Target located. Get to Dalton's room now, we leave in one hour. I replied that I understood."

"What...?" She knew what 'copy' meant, but the rest of it made no sense, even after him telling her what it meant to him.

"Get dressed." He stopped what he was doing, plucked the phone from her hand, turned her toward her bedroom, and patted her tush. "Go, we need to hurry."

Finally, her brain engaged, and she turned and raced across the living room to her bedroom. She didn't have much stuff. Everything she had currently fit into two plastic shopping bags. She stripped off the robe and dropped it on the bed. There was no time for underwear, so she pulled on the sweats. A bra was needed, but the struggle to get it on when her fingers refused to do what she wanted was maddening. "Argh."

"I got you." Rory's fingers took the straps of the bra from her, and she felt them moving against her back as he snapped the hooks closed. He patted her back. "There, you're all set." She covered her boobs with her hands, grabbed a T-shirt, and pulled it on.

"Shoes?"

"There." She nodded toward the door but kept stuffing her clothes into the bags.

"Put these on."

She balanced herself with one hand on his shoulder as she slipped her feet into the Sketchers. "Is he okay?"

"I don't know any more than I told you."

She grabbed the bags off the bed. "Let's go. I'm ready." She moved to go past him to the bedroom door, but stopped when he laid his hand on her arm.

"Whatever this is, we deal with it together, okay?"

She wasn't stupid enough to assume she would be allowed to go with the men and Snow. They would want to stash her somewhere she was safe while they went after Sam. There was no way on the planet that she would jeopardize Sam or any of them by insisting she needed to go too. "Promise you will tell me what's going on."

"I promise." He pressed a fast hard kiss to her lips, grabbed her hand in his, and she had to jog to keep up with him. He grabbed his rucksack and slung it over the opposite shoulder to her.

Adalyn followed him. He appeared to know where he was going. He paused in front of a door with the number four-fifty-two on it and knocked.

"Good, you're here." Jeep opened the door, revealing the whole team and an older gentleman who looked enough like Dalton to be the father he'd mentioned earlier. Both stood in front of a darkened monitor which sat in the middle of the table.

Rory scanned the room, nodded to everyone, and squeezed her fingers with his. "SITREP?"

Research for a previous novel told her he was asking for a situation report.

"Please."

Dalton glanced at Rory, silent communication passing between them that she didn't understand. She opened her mouth, but snapped it shut again when Dalton spoke first.

"Brace yourselves for what you are about to see," he warned. "Snow insists you can handle it."

The last bit was directed at her. "I can handle it." Except she wasn't sure she could if…

"He's alive, but it's not good." Dalton leaned over and pressed a button on the keyboard bringing the monitor to life.

Her hand flew to her mouth when what she was looking at impacted on her heart. Her knees buckled and only Rory's hands kept her on her feet. "Oh my God."

"I'm sorry you have to see this shit," Dalton muttered. "But we don't have time to shield you, and we need Rory or I'd send him with you."

"I'm not going any…"

"You promised," Rory whispered in her ear. "Trust me. Please."

Her son was sitting chained to a bed with a fucking collar around his neck. His beautiful hair, gone. Bruises marred his face. "I'm—I'm okay, go on, keep going."

"We've been running Sam's picture through all of the human traffickers' websites, trying to come up with a match." Dalton's tone was matter of fact, as if he was trying to spare her the worst of it. "Lina gave us the name of one. He's dead, but we were able to link a known associate of his with Kristin Warriner."

Human traffickers.

Oh no. No. No.

"With the help of some other tech gurus, Trev was able to get us a location. But we need to go now. There is an auction tonight. If we can make it before…" Dalton trailed off.

"Why are you still here… go… go…" Why were they waiting? Did they not know how urgent this was? "I'll be fine. Go. Go."

"Dad, this is Adalyn Cassidy," Dalton introduced her to his father. "Adalyn, this is my father; he's going to take you to Italy and ensure your safety before he goes home."

"I can…"

"Dad, we discussed this," Dalton growled. "Once you drop Adalyn in Italy, you are going home."

"Just go already." They were arguing about stupid things. They needed to go for Sam. Now. "I'll send him home from Italy." She had no clue why they were sending her there. And no idea how she was getting there with no passport, but that was something she could worry about later.

Dalton studied her for a heartbeat before he nodded and snapped the laptop closed. He unplugged it from the monitor and stuffed it into a hardbacked case. "Let's roll."

"Be safe," Dalton's father said.

Adalyn turned to Rory. She wasn't expecting the kiss, but she leaned into it. "Be safe, save my son."

"We'll see you in Italy," he promised, and then he was gone, leaving her alone in the hotel room with Mr. Knight Senior.

"Adalyn, isn't it?" Mr. Knight went to the window and pulled back the curtains.

"Yes."

"Come see this."

She had no idea what he meant, but she crossed the room to stand next to him anyway.

"Do you hear it?"

She cocked her head to one side, listening.

Whoop. Whoop. Whoop. Whoop.

"What is that? Is that a helicopter?"

"Yes, it is. A military one," Mr. Knight said. "I don't know how my son arranged it, and I don't think I want to know." As he spoke, the helicopter came into view, hovered, and set down on the lawn below them.

"Wow."

"It's always an amazing sight; keep watching."

There was no way she wasn't going to watch. As soon as the helicopter touched the ground, small figures dressed in black raced out from the side of the hotel and made a beeline for it. The last figure turned around and scanned the building before lifting his hand and giving a thumbs up signal. She knew that was for her. Rory's last promise that he would bring her son back to her. He turned around and jumped into the machine just as it started to lift off the ground again. "Holy cow."

"That was your man telling you it will be okay."

"I know."

They both watched out the window as the helicopter got further and further away.

"How do you do it?"

"Do what, child?"

"Watch him leave?"

"I couldn't for a long time," Mr. Knight admitted. "But then there was an incident in Afghanistan. A chopper much like that one was shot down. I knew he wasn't at base. He'd called the night before and asked how the Dodgers were doing," Mr. Knight explained. "That was our code for he was going on a dangerous job. I spent two days waiting for a knock at the door. One I was so grateful never came, and so guilty that I was relieved my son wasn't one of the thirty-one on board. I promised myself I'd never not watch him again."

Her already broken heart shattered at the pain and fear she heard in the older man's voice.

"Will you take some advice from an old man?"

"Of course." She'd be an idiot not to listen when someone who lived the life of a military family offered her advice.

"Don't let the precious moments pass you by. Don't let fear be what stops you from grabbing it all with both hands."

"Grabbing what?" She thought she knew what he meant, but she needed him to voice it. She needed to be sure she wasn't making a mistake.

"Love, child. Love. Grab it while you can, because before

you know it, the one you love is flying off on a helicopter into a situation and you don't know if they will make it back." Mr. Knight turned to the door when a knock sounded. "Grab the opportunity while you can." He paused to glance out the peephole on the door. "Our ride to Italy is here." He offered her the crook of his arm. "Shall we?"

"Why, yes, kind Sir, we shall." She forced some levity into her voice. This kind gentleman didn't need to know her stomach hated the food she'd eaten earlier. He also didn't need to know that her knees were knocking so hard she was surprised he couldn't hear them. But then, he'd offered her his arm. Maybe he had.

"Bella Italia, here we come."

CHAPTER TWENTY-ONE

Sweat rolled down Rory's back. Even at this altitude on a mountain side near Bobotov Kuk in Montenegro, it was fucking hot. Of course, it was hot. Why wouldn't it be hotter than hell? Mother nature was throwing a temper tantrum, or she forgot to take her menopausal meds and Europe from the Atlantic Coast to the Russian border was experiencing a history making heat wave. He plucked at the material of his camo shirt where it clung to his sides. He kept his eyes trained on the mansion below, just as he had for the last six hours as they waited for the right opportunity to present itself. He watched Dalton click the button on his comms unit, and thankfully, he could hear what was said.

"TOC, Nemesis, anything?"

"Nemesis, TOC," Trev immediately replied. "We are tracking chatter. I'm just waiting on Lina to translate. She had to use the restroom."

"Roger that, TOC."

As much as Rory wanted to growl in frustration that his boss's pregnant wife needed to use the bathroom, there was no way he was stupid enough to do it today. He'd already agreed he would bring them to the location but wouldn't lead the attack.

Rory pinched his fingers into his eyes. He was used to this, damn it. Spending long hours in the field on recon watch was second nature to him. But this time, this mission was different. This time it was Sam on the line. He would not fail Adalyn. They would not fail Sam. The boy was coming home with him, even if he had to march down to the mansion they were watching and knock on the fucking door with a ball of cash in his hand. He'd always hated human traffickers with the burning vengeance of a thousand suns, but today he'd pay those fuckers whatever amount of money they asked for if it meant he got to take Sam home to his mom.

"How are you doing, bro?"

He glanced at Jeep out of the corner of his eye. It wasn't lost on him that their second in command was riding his ass on this mission. Dalton was smart enough to be worried, but he should know he didn't need to. There was no way Rory was going to allow the rage he felt for what had happened to Adalyn and Sam to make him reckless. That wasn't a fucking option. Every instinct he had inside screamed at him that these were the people responsible for hurting his woman and taking Sam from them. The only thing keeping his ass in place and his eyes on the house below was his need to not fuck this up and get Sam and any other children in the house killed. "Just dandy."

"Liar."

"Damn straight," he admitted. "But I swear I'm solid enough not to fuck this up."

"If that changes," Jeep tapped him on the back, "I want to be the first to know."

"Roger that, Sir."

While he understood Jeep checking in on him, it chafed

and rubbed him all kinds of wrong. But he had enough experience in the field to suck it up and deal. He held his breath as he stared through the binoculars, scanning the only road to the house they watched. He clicked his comms unit. "All stations, Six. We have movement approaching our target location from the west."

"Copy," Jeep replied, telling Rory that Dalton was still talking to TOC. "Four, this is Three, do you have eyes on?"

"Three, Four, yes, Sir, I do," Snow replied from her sniper's nest where she had full view of both the road and the mansion. "We have a convoy incoming, five SUVs."

"Copy," Jeep replied. He belly-crawled across the rocks and tapped Dalton on the shoulder.

Shit, five SUVs; that was a few more than they had anticipated. If each vehicle carried four, then they possibly could have at least twenty tangos to go with the ten they had counted already at the house. Not impossible odds, but their mission had gotten just that little bit harder. All the time chatter from his teammates was at a normal level in his ear. He'd mostly learned to filter what was needed and ignore the rest. But today was too important, and he latched onto every piece of information, filing it away in case he needed it.

"One, TOC," Trev hailed Dalton. "We might have a problem."

"Go for One, TOC."

"The intelligence coming out of the local police station says they have a team situated about five klicks to the south. You may have company for your party."

"Three, Four, that convoy is at the two-mile mark," Snow updated them on the position of the vehicles. "TOC, confirmation of that raiding party. They just took the turn off the trail head."

"Roger. Three, copy that."

"TOC, copies."

Over and back the information flew, keeping all of them updated on where the players were at any given time.

"TOC, One, recommendations?"

Shit, Dalton is asking if we execute or retreat.

FUUUUCK!

He covered his mouth with one gloved hand as he silently screamed the curse in his head. The last thing he wanted was for that to echo down the mountain.

"One, TOC, scrub that intel packet you have, stat," Trev ordered. "I have an idea. But I need at least two minutes to put it in place."

"Copy, TOC." Dalton pulled up the flap of his flak jacket and pulled out some paper. Using his gloved fingers, he ripped off all printer IP markers and the Nemesis logo. He handed the papers to Jeep to double-check and stuffed the scraps he'd torn off into one of the pouches on his belt.

"It's good." Jeep handed him back the papers, and Dalton shoved them into the side pocket on his camo pants.

"TOC, One, data has been sanitized."

"Copy, One," Trev replied. "If I buy you an extra five minutes, can you do a snatch and grab of our principle?"

"Depends on how much you want me to clean house."

"I'm thinking lockdown as a gift to our friendly local police, and we get Sonic out of there before he gets tied up in a shit load of red tape."

YES. I love that idea. Let's do that.

Rory held his breath as Dalton and Jeep exchanged glances. When Jeep nodded, Rory did an internal fist-bump.

Thank fuck!

"One, use non-lethal force as much as possible," Trev warned. "We do not want to have to call in favors to get your asses clear of shit unless absolutely necessary."

"TOC, Four," Snow interrupted. "Our convoy has come to a stop about half a klick from the house."

"Four, TOC, that's on me," Trev confirmed. "When you have an all-electric vehicle and everything hooked up to places it shouldn't be, then you get hackers who can tell your SUV it's out of juice and boom, oops, your vehicle stops and won't move until someone overrides the hack."

"Thank fuck you're on our side, TOC," Snow muttered. "Umm, TOC, they have pulled out a jenny and are plugging it in."

Kinda ironic to be using what was probably a diesel-powered generator to recharge an electric vehicle. But Rory didn't care about ironies and shit, he was just grateful Trev had bought them some extra time.

Dalton pulled a map of the property out and they huddled around it. Within two minutes they'd adjusted their mission plan to a snatch, grab, and retreat. The entry points were already marked as was the location they hoped to find Sam, aka code name Sonic, in. During planning en route to Montenegro, Dalton had called his father to get a word or phrase Sam would recognize as only coming from her.

"TOC, One, waiting on your call, brother."

Even though Dalton ran Nemesis Inc. with an iron fist, when it came to making the mission calls based off intel, Trev in the tactical operations center at home had the final say. They'd found by keeping their protocols similar to how they'd worked when in the military, it caused less errors.

"All Stations, the electric fence is dead and all systems are down."

"TOC, One, confirm orders."

"Execute, execute, execute."

Rory eased from his hiding place, keeping his weapon at ready position. He ran toward the house in formation with his team. They made sure to stay behind cover as much as possible to ensure they wouldn't be spotted through any of the windows. Trev had already taken care of the electrical system and the backup security systems.

When they reached the house, he put his back to the wall with Logan on his six and inched his way toward the back of the property. Dalton and Jeep mirrored their positions and went toward the front where the biggest threat of being seen was.

His heart was pounding as he snuck a look around the corner, ensuring the way was clear before he moved fully around to the back of the house. In his ear he could hear the clicks from Dalton and Jeep confirming they, too, were making progress. Good... maybe the bastards wouldn't realize shit was going down until it was too late.

Logan tapped on his shoulder, his signal to proceed, and they approached the back door. He waited for a count of three before he reached out one gloved hand to check if it was locked. He and Logan exchanged glances when it gave under his hand.

Jeez, you'd think these shitheads would be a bit more wary considering they are selling kids.

But was he going to be mad about human traffickers who felt secure enough to leave their back door wide open? Hell no, he wasn't. He and Logan made their way without confrontation through the house to a door which the floor plans on his wrist-held computer said led further into the house. This was where the most danger would be. They would be in a less than secure position, with the possibility of being trapped in the crossfire if the tangos ran this way when Dalton and Jeep entered from the front of the house.

"Tango One, secured."

Jeep's confirmation came just as he and Logan entered the service hallway off the kitchen.

"Six, One, Tango Two is headed your way."

"Copy that, One." He winced when the floorboard

creaked under his foot. "Even the fucking house wants to give our location away," he muttered almost silently under his breath.

"Keep going," Logan whispered. "I've got your six."

Rory paused to listen with his head cocked to the side. How could there be at least fourteen children under twelve in this house and there not be any noise? Any time he'd been around even one or two kids of that age there had been noise. Football games, video games, arguments, hell, even some knockdown, all hell letting loose, fist fights, and that was just his nieces taking no shit from the boys.

"All stations, Four," Snow called through comms. "Be advised, our local friendly cops will make contact with our stalled tangos in about thirty seconds."

"Copy," Logan replied for them both.

He and Logan continued through the house, silently clearing rooms as they followed the floor plans to the room they had pinpointed as being the most likely location for the kids. It just fucking sucked that they wouldn't be able to rescue all of the kids.

Rat tat tat...

The sound of rapid-fire gunshots could be heard even with the distance between the house and where the convoy had stalled out. Immediately he could hear the sound of running footsteps.

Logan tapped on his right arm and Rory stepped to the side, taking cover in the door of the room they'd just cleared. The footsteps got closer and closer. While their mission was to use non-lethal force if at all possible, Rory was so damn tempted to shoot the bastard. He'd never know what hit him. But doing so would require paperwork and may jeopardize the mission. Saving Sam was his top priority.

He glanced at Logan and raised his fist, making a punching motion. The corners of Logan's lips curled upward, and he nodded, his response clear even without the words being spoken. *Hell, yes, punch the fucker.*

The man raced past the room door, and he didn't have time to see or figure out what happened. Rory pulled his side arm, made sure the safety was on, and slammed it into the back of the asshole's head. The man slumped and Rory grabbed him by the back of the shirt, dragging him back into the room. He and Logan made short work of securing him to a chair.

"Should we check his pulse?"

"Hell no, if that love tap did more than knock him out and give him a concussion, it serves him right."

"Let's go." Logan gestured for him to move. "Our target room should be around the next corner."

"All Stations, you have five minutes to exfil."

Rory put on a burst of speed, all the while maintaining his vigilance. Just as they had suspected, the new hallway revealed a door with a chair in the hallway outside of it. "TOC, Five and Six approaching Jackpot."

"Copy."

With Logan keeping watch on his six, Rory reached into one of his many pockets for his picking kit and bent to the door. Just in case, he tried the handle. *Fucking dumbasses*, the door opened. *How the hell is it not even locked?* He cautiously pushed it open a crack. The door immediately slammed closed again with force.

"Ouch, my fucking nose." Pain streaked through his face. He touched his nose with the back of his hand and winced. "Fucker broke my nose." He pushed against the door again. He could feel the resistance of someone pushing against it but didn't have time to knock and ask politely if Sam Cassidy could come out to play. He put his shoulder to the door and gave a hard shove. The door gave and he stepped into the room with his weapon at ready position. He made damn sure to keep his fingers away from the trigger. The last thing he wanted to do was cause an accident.

His eyes widened when he caught sight of the group of boys. All of them looked scared and one little hellion with a shaved head stood in front of the rest, glaring at them.

"If you don't let us go, my momma will make you pay. I fucking swear it. She will never stop looking for me." The boy lifted his face, giving Rory and Logan the first full look at his features. His pupils were huge in his eyes, and a single tear ran from the corner of his eye down one cheek, yet he didn't step back or give ground.

"Sam." He clicked on his comms unit. "TOC, Six, I have Sonic. I repeat, I have Sonic."

"Copy that," Trev replied. "Get your asses outta there, Stat."

"How do you know that name?" Sam swallowed hard. He wiped the snot from his nose with the back of his arm. "Who told you that name?"

Relief slammed into Rory when Sam's words confirmed it. "Your momma sent me." He spoke fast. "The cops are coming in, but we gotta go now if we want to avoid being here for days while they figure shit out."

"Liar."

"I swear it."

Sam spread his arms wide and pushed the other boys behind him, herding them backward into the corner. Smart kid. Put a wall to your back and you are clear to face what's in front of you. "Prove it."

"Grab him," Logan ordered. "We gotta go. Now."

Rory didn't want to scare the shit out of him. He also didn't want to traumatize him any more than he already had. "TOC, Six, patch in Sonic's mom, stat."

"Six, TOC, no promises."

"If she says you come with me, will you do it without screaming?"

"Maybe."

How the hell is this kid only eight years old? He has more street smarts than most teenagers.

"Six, TOC, that's a negative. We don't have time, grab the target and hot foot it, stat."

Fuck, he'd been afraid of that. He secured his weapon with his battle sling and grabbed Sam. "Sorry, kid. I'll get your mom on the line as soon as it's safe."

"Police are coming," Logan told the other children. "I promise they are right here. You are going home too."

Sam wriggled and kicked. Twice he came within screeching distance of Rory's balls. "Settle down." The long walk from the room to their exit point was the longest journey Rory ever remembered taking. That fucking hallway had grown since they'd cleared each room less than ten minutes ago. He was fucking sure of it. "Shit." Tears filled his eyes when Sam managed to get his teeth into the hand covering his mouth. But he didn't dare let go. A scream now would alert the police to their presence.

"One and Three coming up on your six," Dalton warned just before he and Jeep joined him, Logan, and Sam. "Move it. There's a cop right on our asses."

Rory tucked Sam under his arm like he would a sack of feed and picked up his speed. Running with your hand over a kid's mouth as you tried to keep him quiet wasn't as easy as it seemed. How the hell criminals did this day in day out was beyond him. Especially when that kid was still fighting with everything he had in him.

"Pass him here," Dalton ordered when they reached the fence. "We need to go over, because if we cut it, they know where we went out."

"The second I lift my hand, he's gonna scream."

"Not if he wants to see his momma tomorrow he won't," Dalton growled.

"Six, TOC, I've got your lady."

God fucking bless him. "I fucking love you, Trev." Rory whipped off his comms unit. It wasn't protocol, and Dalton may boot his ass for it later, but it was the quickest way. "Tell Trev my comms is in Sonic's ear."

Dalton scowled at him but did as he asked while Rory struggled to get the earpiece in place. "Damn it, kid, I'm trying to get you to hear your mom." He didn't know why the kid believed him, but he snatched the earpiece and pushed it in his ear. The little bastard didn't let go of the hold he had on his hand with his teeth while he did it either. When Sam burst into tears and finally let his hand free, Rory handed him off to Dalton, jumped the fence, and hauled Sam over. This time he scooped him up into his arms and bolted for cover with the guys hot on his heels.

"TOC, One, we are passing checkpoint Rodeo." Dalton gave Trev the 'we're out and headed for our extraction point' intel.

We fucking did it. We have him.
Yes!

CHAPTER TWENTY-TWO

IT TRULY WAS beautiful here in this part of Italy. Who would have thought the US had control of an Italian island? Adalyn looked out over the beautiful landscaping. This sure looked like some kind of military base, but nobody would tell her anything.

She'd arrived with Dalton's father, been introduced to someone called Zenko who'd threatened to drop a glitter bomb on her head if she caused trouble, shown to this little guest house, and more or less been left to her own devices.

She tapped her pen off the pad and reached for her iced water. Without a computer and no access to anything, she had nothing to do but write. "How the hell am I supposed to write when I don't know what's happening?"

Did they find Sam?
Is he okay?
Is he hurt?
Scared?
How in the name of buttered toast do people do this all the time?
She wasn't even sure why she was bothering to try and

write. She didn't know if she could ever come back from this fuck-up.

"Stop that. Your readers are awesome. They've got your back. They always have. They always will."

Say that louder for the idiot who's doubting it in your head.

Repeat it. Multiple times.

I have the best and most awesome readers.

They have my back.

Her head shot up at the sound of an approaching vehicle. She'd been expecting one of the golf carts which had been used to get her from the main building to this guest house. She stood out of the chair and leaned her hands on the fence railing surrounding the little cobblestone patio space she'd been sitting in. "What in the world is that?" She'd never seen a three-wheel mini truck before. She gaped at it with her mouth open as it sped down the track. The driver's head was out the window as if he didn't quite fit in the truck, and he steered with one hand. She had no clue what he was doing with the pedals or how he was changing gears. But based on the whining from the engine, he probably wasn't changing the gears at all.

She took a step back when the three-wheel truck screeched to a stop in front of her guest house.

"Get in!" the driver yelled. "Costa needs you on the phone, stat."

She heard Rory and phone and bolted to the gate in her bare feet. Thankfully, her yard had been in the shade for the last couple of hours and she didn't scald the skin off her feet as she ran. "Sam?"

"No idea." The man barely waited for her to jump in, closing the door, that he didn't wait for before he drove the truck straight up onto the lawn and turned them back toward the main house.

"Eeep." She leaned one hand on the dashboard and tugged the door shut before it whipped open again.

"Sorry, time crunch," the man muttered.

She couldn't see anything past his chest as his head and shoulders were completely out of the truck.

"Want me to change the gears?" She leaned forward as much as she could. "You are hitting red numbers on the dial thingy."

"Fuck, yes, please," he grunted. "Gimme a sec, I need to hit the other pedal." He moved one leg and the truck jerked almost to a stop. "Shit, wrong one, sorry. I can't see where my feet are from here." His leg moved again. "Pull it straight back."

She grabbed the gear stick and did as he asked. Thankfully, the truck did what it was meant to do and the dial moved down a notch from the red. "I think you need to go up another gear."

"No need, we're just around the corner."

"That's not an Irish corner, is it?" She couldn't resist asking. "Where around the corner could mean anything from 'right around the very next corner', or the next one about three miles away?"

"Hah, you sound like…" He trailed off and the truck lurched to a stop. "Stupid ape."

"Excuse me. What on earth are you calling me names for?"

"Not you, the truck." He snorted. "These trucks are called *Apes*, and I'm convinced Max got them as torture devices."

Zenko appeared at her side of the truck. "Ma'am, you gotta come with me fast." He opened the door and practically tugged her out. "Run."

"What happened? Is Sam okay?" She ran after him as fast as her bare feet would allow her. "Ow, shit." She had forgotten the gravel they had in front of the main building.

"Why didn't you say you had no shoes on?" Zenko glanced at her feet, scowled, and picked her up.

"Hey, help me out of the truck."

"I'll be back in a minute, Boss!" Zenko yelled. "I'll just drop our guest with Max first."

"You're an asshole, Marks!" his boss yelled.

"Will you get in trouble?"

"Nah." Zenko placed her on her feet. "What will get me in shit is the photos I take and send to all the guys." He urged her down the stairs and into an underground room. "Here, Max, I need to go rescue Noble from the Ape."

"Take pictures *and* video," the man Zenko had called Max said over his shoulder as he waved her forward. "I need you to tell your kid that Rory is one of the good guys, and I need you to do it fast because they're running."

"They have him?" She wasn't going to believe it until she heard or saw him. It would destroy her for this to be a mistake.

"Yes." Max picked up a headset. "Trev, I have Costa's woman. She has a headset."

"Adalyn?" the voice she recognized as Trev's spoke in her ear.

"Yes…"

"Six, TOC, I've got your lady," Trev said. "Ma'am, I'm patching you through."

"I…"

Max tapped a button near her ear. "Now you can talk to your son."

"Hello? Hello, Sam, can you hear me? Can you hear mommy?" She didn't know what she'd been expecting, or rather what she'd been hoping for, but the sharp inhale of a breath and the sweet, sweet sound of Sam crying in her ear hadn't been it. She slumped forward, bracing her hands on the table in front of her. "Sam, baby. It's Mom. I love you. I love you."

"Here sit down." A chair touched the back of her knees. "If you faint or something, I'm not having Costa wreaking up my computers."

"Mom," Sam sobbed in her ear. "Mommy."

"I'm here," she reassured him. "My friend Rory has you. He's bringing you to me. I promise."

Max tapped her elbow and gestured toward his computer screen. "I've got visual now too."

Her heart almost stopped when she caught a glimpse of Sam. She swallowed down the lump in her throat at the sight of his shorn hair. "I can see you, baby. Keep holding onto Rory. I promise he'll keep you safe."

"He's not Rory," Sam whispered. "They keep calling him Six."

"Tell him that's his call sign," Max said. "Like Batman."

"Do you remember how Bruce Wayne is called Batman?"

"Yeah?"

"Rory is Six like Bruce Wayne is Batman."

"Six is a stupid name." Sam's voice was distorted and the screen she was watching jumped around a lot.

"Baby, he can be called Fairy Princess or whatever he wants as long as he's bringing you back to me."

"We're gonna lose comms in a minute," Max said.

"What? No."

"Mommy..."

"It's okay, baby." She struggled to keep her voice calm. She didn't need to scare him any more than he already was.

"They are being picked up by a helicopter," Max told her softly. "I can't guarantee communication will hold until they are back on the ground."

Oh, no. But also, oh, yes. He was getting out of there.

"You are going to fly on a chopper, Sam. Isn't that so

cool?" She could be excited for him. Sam loved every machine with wings. This was not how either of them had envisioned their first helicopter ride. That was meant to be over the Grand Canyon. But this one she'd pay every single dime she had to make sure he was on that chopper. "I'm so jealous. It's going to be so awesome."

Max clicked something with his mouse and the screen split in two. One side still showed her part of Sam and the ground as Rory ran. The other side of the screen was obviously from someone else's body cameras, as she could see a black dot which was growing bigger and bigger by the second. "When you get on the helicopter, I'm going to have to hang up, okay?"

"No, Moooom."

"I promise I am waiting for you." She slapped away the tears which leaked from her eyes. "You are coming here to me. I promise." She nudged Max. "How long?"

He'd obviously been listening to the conversation, too, as he immediately answered, "The flight on that bird and then a fishing boat straight to here."

"You are getting to go on a fishing boat too!" she exclaimed as if it was the most exciting news on the planet. "You will love it. Maybe you will catch some fish for me to make you fish dippers when you get here."

"Okay." Sam's sniffling told her he didn't think it was okay at all. But at least his sobs were down to soft hiccups.

"I love you," she told him. "I love you so much. Never forget it."

"Love you, Mommy."

CHAPTER TWENTY-THREE

"How are you doing, Sonic?" Rory kept pushing, one step at a time, moving in sync with his team as they worked their way around the mountain. For once he was grateful for all those ten-mile rucks through the Hindu Kush while lugging weapons and gear. Typically, his feet would be screaming at him, because no matter how much you trained when you walked or jogged for miles in combat boots, your feet paid the price. This time if his feet fell off, he would keep moving forward on the stubs which remained.

"Okay." Sam gave him a thumbs up.

Rory was so freaking grateful someone had been able to get Adalyn on the line. It was one thing to run with a sixty-pound boy in your arms, but it would be a whole different ball game to do that when the boy was wriggling and fighting him all the way.

"Our ride is inbound, Six," Dalton warned. "Get ready as we're hoisting up."

"Copy, Sir." The last fucking thing he wanted to do was strap Sam and him into a harness and clip it to a rope, swinging off the ass end of a helo. But he sure as heck wasn't going to refuse the ride out of here either.

As they approached a ridge line, he shifted Sam in his arms and crouched low to prevent sky-lining himself. He could already hear the whoop of the rotors. Even though they were out of view of the mansion and the police, whoever was flying in here to give them a ride out was taking a risk. One he'd owe them a gratitude for. They scooted over the ridge and down a steep slope, bringing them into a small rocky valley. The scattered field of rocks in front of him confirmed why they had to be lifted out. There wasn't the space the size of a sixpence for the bird to land on. "We're going to be flying in a minute, Sam."

"Mommy said that."

He hadn't noticed that Sam had stopped talking.

Rory stopped next to where Jeep was digging into Dalton's ruck. He winced when he saw the harness. "This is not my favorite activity on the planet."

"Want me to take him?" Dalton asked.

"No." Sam's fingers immediately bunched into the straps on his vest. "No."

"Shh, Sam." Rory ran his hand up and down his back. "I got you. We just gotta put a harness on and strap you to my chest, okay? I'm gonna need you to hold onto me like a monkey."

"Huh?"

"You know, arms around my neck, and your legs around my waist." He stepped his legs into the harness, allowing Jeep and Dalton to make sure it was secure. "We're gonna fly like a bird for a bit."

"Higher than the mountain?"

The helo finally hovered over them, rotor wash sending dust and small rocks flying through the air. "Into the sky." Rory adjusted Sam and encouraged him to hold on tight.

Dalton used some parachute cord to secure Sam to Rory's chest.

The shuffle to get close enough to the hoist sent down from the helo was a little awkward, but Jeep held him steady, and Dalton clipped them in.

"Ready to fly?" He raised his voice to be heard over the helo.

"Yess."

He sounds excited. Thank you, sweet baby Jesus.

They were swept off their feet as the hoist retracted, similar to a rescue or medivac helo but without the basket.

"Oh."

Sam buried his face into the crook of Rory's neck. Rory kept one hand under his butt, supporting him, and the other was wrapped tightly around the wire. It took five billion lifetimes to make it from the ground to the feet of the bird. He frowned in confusion when he came face-to-face with Mike, the former SEAL who'd been medically retired after his capture and subsequent rescue. A good friend of Dalton and Jeep's, he'd been spending a lot of time at the ranch lately.

Hands pulled him and Sam into the bird, unhooked the hoist, and sent it back down for the others. Rory shuffled on his knees across the floor of the helo, keeping himself and Sam out of the way while the rest of his team were brought on board. "How are you doing, buddy?"

Sam pulled his face out of Rory's neck and looked around. "Wow, just wow."

"Yeah, it is kinda wow, isn't it?" He could totally see why a little boy would be enthralled by this. What kid didn't want to play soldiers and fly on helicopters? "Just wait until we swoop left or right..." He rocked Sam first to the left and then to the right. "It feels like your belly is going to fly right out the window."

"Awesome."

It didn't take long for the rest of his team to get their asses off the ground. All took a place on the floor of the bird, surrounding him and Sam while Mike slammed the door shut. He pointed to the headsets. "Seats we don't have, comms we do. Put them on. I gotta help Cas fly this puppy." Mike pointed to the man in the pilot's seat. Rory knew there had been a thing between them before Mike had been captured. The pair of them had been dancing around each other and fucking things up since Mike got back. If they were here causing trouble together, maybe that was a good start. "If he fucks up this bus we took for a joyride, we're gonna have some 'splaining to do to the Greeks."

"What the hell are you telling me, Mike? Did you steal this bird?"

Rory bit down on his bottom lip and buried his face against the side of Sam's head. There was no way he wanted Dalton to transfer his attention to him. Mike was going to be in the cockpit and out of the way of Dalton in full-on Nemesis mode. Laughing out loud at the outrage on his boss's face would be a stupid thing to do right now. "Get ready to swoop," he warned Sam as the helo rose higher into the air.

"We sure did." Mike grinned over his shoulder as he strapped himself into the copilot seat. "It was sitting around doing nothing at the NATO training we were doing. Nobody took it up all week." He twisted dials and adjusted his headset. "Besides, we couldn't let all y'all have all the fun."

"Assholes." Dalton slumped back against the side of the bird. "Do you have any idea how much paperwork you just caused me?"

"Enough to keep your ass at home until your kid is born?" Mike deadpanned. "At least I hope so."

"Fabulous," Dalton muttered. "This was my wife's hair-brained idea?"

"Well, kinda," Castiel answered this time. "She was complaining to Mike that her back and feet hurt when he called to check on her. We decided it was time to give you a head start on getting your butt home, as one of the boys told us that's the first sign she's getting ready to drop the kid."

"I dare you to tell my wife that all y'all are discussing her giving birth in terms of goats and kids."

That was when Rory lost it. The laugh escaped just as the helo banked to the right, turning them toward their destination. Thankfully, his guffaw of laughter was smothered by Sam's squeal of delight.

"We're gonna drop you in a blank spot near the base we were training out of," Castiel said. "It's probably better that we don't arrive there with you as cargo, or there'll be more paperwork."

"Yeah, please don't give me more paperwork," Dalton agreed.

"I don't think this round of it is on you," Castiel said. "I work for Noble, remember? And Mike, well, Mike is Mike, but not under your command."

"Asshole." Mike swatted at Castiel.

"They're funny." Sam nudged him with his elbow. "But my mom is going to be looking for bars of soap to wash their mouths out for saying too many of those bad words."

"These words are for when your mom is not around, okay?" Rory warned. "I don't want her coming after me with a stick for teaching you all of them."

"I'll just blame him." Sam pointed to Dalton. "It seems like he's supposed to be the boss, so it's his fault."

It was a good thing he hadn't been eating or drinking or he'd had spit out whatever had been in his mouth for sure. "I love you, kid. You're freaking awesome."

"My mom says that too."

Dalton spluttered and muttered under his breath, but his

hand reached out and he patted Sam's back, letting them know he wasn't mad with him.

"Someone will have trucks waiting for you when we land," Mike said. "Not great trucks, but trucks which will get you to the coast. From there you do fishing boat to Isole della Magdalena."

"Roger that," Dalton replied. "I'll take it. Thanks."

"You're welcome," Castiel muttered. "Remember that when Noble is bitching to you about paperwork."

"Hah."

―――

"Are you good to walk, Sam, or do you want me to give you a piggyback?" Rory ducked low to make sure he didn't get his head chopped off by the rotors. He could shuffle his gear around if he had to and make room for Sam on his back.

"I can walk." Sam held onto him, his fingers still twisted into Rory's vest as he found his ground feet after the flight. "How far?"

"About a mile." Jeep smiled at Sam. "Then we get in trucks and go to the sea."

"And then a boat?"

"Yes." Jeep nodded. "But maybe we need to find you some clothespins for your nose as it's gonna be smelly, because it's a fishing trawler."

"Will you be wearing a clothespin on your nose?"

Jeep waggled his eyebrows. "Maybe."

"Okay, if Rory is too, then I want one."

"Here." Snow pulled the ball cap she kept in her ruck for times when she couldn't wear a helmet and placed it backward on Sam's head. "There, now you have camo, too, and look like part of the team."

Rory refused to make a big deal out of Snow's gesture.

She wasn't the most approachable person, and she sure had her quirks. But she was one hell of a sniper, and if she gave you her word, she kept it, even if it made her look like an asshole. It made Rory's heart swell to see these gruff people he worked with doing their best to make Sam feel part of the team. To show him he was one of theirs, at least for now. He nodded in thanks to Jeep, but Snow had already gone ahead, probably to scout out their way, making sure they were safe, taking his role so he could stay with Sam.

"It's hot."

"It sure is, buddy." He glanced at his wrist-held computer and tapped a few buttons. "It's about one hundred degrees, see..." He tilted his arm to show Sam the numbers. "Ninety-nine point five." Behind them, the helo lifted back into the air. He waved at Castiel and Mike.

"Let's go." Dalton moved them toward the edge of the field they'd landed in. "We gotta stick to this track for about a mile. The trucks will be there waiting for us at the end."

"Awesome." Rory moved Sam's hand from his vest, shouldered his ruck, and caught Sam's fingers with his. "On the road again..."

"Don't sing, Mr. Six," Sam whispered as a flock of crows lifted from a nearby tree. "You're scaring the birds."

"Brat." He grinned as they walked toward the trucks. "I'm telling your momma."

"She's going to be so happy to see me that she's going to be too busy crying to hear you."

"He's got you there, Ro." Logan sidestepped a cow patty.

"Yes, he does." And Rory didn't even care. She could cry all she wanted as long as they were happy tears. Those he could take, the other kind not so much. "Man, it's hot."

"And the trucks have no aircon," Snow informed them as they neared two rickety pickup trucks. "I started the engines, hoping to take the heat down a notch or two, but they're blowing hot air."

"Dang it. Boss, if we pass a store, we're gonna have to pick up some frozen peas or something, because we're gonna die from heat stroke in there."

"Yeah, we can do that." Dalton started breaking down his weapons. Whoever had provided the trucks had been thoughtful enough to provide them with a couple of empty duffel bags. They all stashed their gear and within five minutes they were in the hellishly hot vehicles, with their noses pointed toward the coast.

Finally, Rory could breathe a little easier. He was on track to keep his promise to Adalyn. He had her son, next stop the boat, and the one after that Isole della Magdalena.

"Hooyah!" Dalton yelled as they flew over a humpback bridge and the truck lifted off the road.

"Never mind, hooyah, you idiot." Jeep punched Dalton. "Keep the damn truck on the road or explain to the girls why we're all injured when we get back."

Yup, all was currently right in his world. The bosses were bickering, Logan and Snow were on their sixes, and he had Adalyn's kid sleeping on his shoulder. It was time to get their butts home and figure out the rest.

CHAPTER TWENTY-FOUR

Two days later

ADALYN KNEW she shouldn't be out here in the hottest part of the day. But she couldn't see the dock from her little guest house. She put the binoculars she'd borrowed from Max to her eyes and scanned the horizon again. "Where are you?"

"They'll be here when they get here."

"Eep." She jumped a mile when Noble spoke behind her. "Don't do that; make some noise."

"Sorry, habit." Noble stepped up to the barrier which ran along in front of the dock. "They will be coming in today, but you have time to eat some lunch first." He placed his hand on the binoculars and lowered them. "Seriously, standing out here isn't going to make them appear any faster."

"I know, but…"

"Nope, if you have heat stroke when they get here, I'm not explaining to your kid why you're sick."

"You really are an asshole, aren't you?"

"So they tell me." Noble pointed to the big black truck parked a little further away. "But either way, put yourself in my truck and come eat food and drink some water at the house."

"What? No Ape today?"

His cheeks reddened, and she totally got why. She'd seen the video footage of him stuck in the window of the truck, which Zenko had taken while she was talking to Sam.

He took the binoculars from her and headed toward his truck, clearly expecting her to follow him. "I'm banning those damn Apes off the island."

"I don't know that you can ban them off the whole island." She climbed into the passenger side and immediately sighed in relief as the blast of cold air hit her. "Wow, that aircon is nice."

"Right?" He tossed the glasses onto the back seat. "At least here I can leave it running, because if someone steals my truck on this base, shit's gonna fly."

"I may have to keep it for the aircon alone."

"After I've been so nice to you?"

"Totally, because it will be Zenko's fault." She'd learned these two squabbled like little boys, but it appeared to be some kind of love language for them. Her books and storylines were going to be so much stronger after spending these past few days here on their base.

"Everything is Zenko's fault." Noble pulled to a stop in a shaded carport in front of the main building.

"Please tell me it's something cold for lunch." She had no business complaining about what they gave her to eat. Especially because she wasn't being charged a thing for it. "Because if it isn't, then you and me are going to have problems."

"Nah, it's just cold cuts, cheese, and bruschetta," Noble promised. "If I dare turn on an oven, I think Max would shoot me."

"I'd help." She followed him into a surprisingly homey Italian country kitchen. Pots and pans hung on racks over the stove, and beautiful hand painted tiles covered the backsplash. "Wow."

"Nice, isn't it?" He grinned at her. "I love this room."

"And you didn't want me to redecorate when we moved in here." Max appeared from the hallway leading to where she knew his office was. "Now it's your favorite room in the house."

"Yup." Noble nodded seriously. "You took a military base and made it a home for us and our people."

"Flatterer, what are you after?" Max grabbed a large jug of iced tea from the fridge, filled it with ice from the machine on the counter, and placed it in the middle of the table. "There's no way you are complimenting my design skills after all the muttering and bitching you were doing when I was showing you plans."

These two are freaking adorable.

She'd figured out pretty quick that Noble and Max were a couple. If she now had the notion in her head for a protector romance with a power couple at the helm of a special task force, well it was all Rory and Dalton's fault for sending her here to a place where there was so much fodder for her imagination.

"Sit, sit." Noble pulled out a chair for her. "Help yourself; we don't stand on ceremony when it's just family."

Color her confused. "But I'm not family."

"Yeah, you kinda are." Max pointed his fork at her. "You belong to Costa, Costa is Luc's team brother, so that makes you family and us your big brothers."

"Oh, I see where this is going… you're going to give Rory crap, aren't you?"

"Damn straight." Max stuffed his loaded fork into his mouth.

"We appreciate the opportunity to give any Nemesis team

member shit," Noble agreed. "But we'd do it anyway, because it's all kinds of fun."

She shook her head at them. They were enjoying this way too much. She'd always assumed these types of alpha males were tough, gruff, and reserved. They could be, she'd seen that when she'd first arrived. But the more time she spent with them all, the more she saw them for the down to earth, fun-loving family who loved to pull pranks and make fun of each other. Now those traits... Those were definitely making it into future books. The only problem was, she wasn't entirely sure her readers would think it was plausible. But she'd figure out a way to make them believe it. "Do we know how much longer for them to get here?" She sampled a piece of wonderful mozzarella, then cut another piece, added a tomato on top, followed by a drizzle of olive oil, and popped it into her mouth.

Mmh, yummy.

"It will probably be closer to dark," Max said. "They are fishing a couple of nautical miles out."

"Fishing?" She almost choked on her mouthful of food. "Why are they fishing?"

"Jeez, woman, don't shriek." Noble stuck his finger in the ear nearest her and wriggled it. "They are on a commercial trawler and need a reason to come to the dock. We don't want the Coast Guard paying attention."

Max grinned at Noble. "You mean you don't want to add to that pile of paperwork I just put on your desk for Cas and Mike borrowing the helo... right?" He dragged out the last word.

"Hell no, no more paperwork," Noble grumbled. "I already have the consulate in Rome working on emergency passports for you and Sam."

"Oh." She was totally being ungrateful and she knew it. "I'm sorr—"

"Don't you dare finish that sentence," Max ordered. "Saving the innocent and fixing shit is our jam. But we gotta make sure everyone is safe while we do it."

"I appreciate all you've done for me and Sam."

"We know." Noble pushed the plate of bruschetta closer. "Try the cheese with this, it will blow your mind. Sam will be here soon enough."

"Thank you." She did as he'd ordered, but the wonderful food now tasted like sawdust, no doubt colored by her disappointment that it was taking so long for her son to be returned to her. However, she was grateful, so grateful he was alive and coming back to her. Disappointment, she could live with for now.

"Careful you don't fall over the railing," Zenko warned.

"I won't." She was almost bouncing in excitement and understood his concern. From the second Max had told her the trawler was coming into view she'd been almost beside herself. Noble, Max, Zenko, and a couple of people she didn't recognize all lined up along the railing, flanking her on either side, ready to celebrate Sam's safe return with her. "Hurry, hurry, hurry."

"No, please don't hurry or that boat will be sitting on our laps before we can say 'watch out.'"

"That doesn't sound fun at all."

"As someone who's lugged boats on my shoulders all the way down a freaking beach in California," Zenko muttered. "Let me tell you, it's not fun to have a boat sitting on your head."

"Ouch, that sounds more like hell than fun."

"Why do you think it's called hell week?"

Oh, now it made so much more sense. She'd been starting

to think he was just cray-cray. But hell week was what made SEALs, which totally fit Zenko Marks.

"Mom."

The faint sound of Sam's voice had her scanning the boat. She could just about make out the shape of someone waving at her. "Sam!" she yelled back as loud as she could, waving one arm in the air while jumping up and down in the spot.

"I'm so excited. Sue me."

"Hah." He bunched his hand into the back of her T-shirt as if she was going to dive into the water and start swimming toward Sam.

"I'm not jumping in the sea."

"I'm just making sure of that," Zenko replied. "I'm not getting shit from Costa for not looking after you good enough."

The closer the boat came, the more she could make out the figures of the people on board. Rory stood with Sam in front of him, his arms making sure her boy didn't take a nosedive into the water. It took forever, but the trawler finally came alongside the dock. "Oh my God, his hair."

"His hair will grow back," Zenko said. "He's here, he's safe. Take the win—enjoy it—worry about the rest later."

He was right, she knew he was. But how did she answer Sam when he asked her if Sonic was still Sonic when his spikes were gone? She didn't have time to figure it out right now and as soon as the gangplank was down, she bolted toward the boat, Sam, and Rory.

CHAPTER TWENTY-FIVE

"Brace, Sam," Rory warned. "Your mom is coming in at Mach speed." He'd had to keep a tight hold on Sam for the last half hour. As soon as he'd spotted Adalyn on the dock he'd wanted to jump in and swim to her. Seeing as Rory didn't know if Sam could swim or not, he'd refused, much to his little charge's chagrin.

"Mom!" Sam yelled.

"It's a good thing we finished fishing a couple of miles back." Rory picked him up so he could see Adalyn better. "Or we'd have sent every fish within a hundred miles swimming for one of the deep trenches." He grinned at Sam's excitement. Over the last two days, the little boy had clung to him. He showed flashes of her personality to the others, but with him he was throwing down snark like it was going out of style and Rory loved it.

He carried Sam down the ramp, knowing the guys would get his gear just as he would have for them if the shoe was on the other foot. He placed Sam on his feet as he reached the dock and let him run.

"Sam."

"Mommy."

Sam slammed into Adalyn's body and she dropped to her knees with her arms wrapped around her son. He couldn't hear what they were saying, but the sight of them together made even his normally cold dead heart feel an emotion. No, that wasn't right, it was more than an emotion, it was a whole bunch of them slamming into his heart one after the other.

"This right here is why we do what we do."

"Yeah, Boss, yeah, it is." He knew he was just standing here like an idiot, but he couldn't make himself move away. He never wanted to stop looking at scenes like this. Adalyn's arms were wrapped around Sam's back. He knew letting go of her child again was something she'd never want to do. He could see by the way Sam was moving that he was crying. When Adalyn lifted her head and stared directly at him, the tears rolling down her cheeks almost brought him to his knees. How the hell could this woman and this child call to places deep inside him he'd never known existed?

"Rory." He didn't hear her voice but recognized the shape of his name on her lips. She held one hand out to him. He didn't need a second invitation. He strode toward them and placed one hand on Sam's back, warning him he was there. "It's just me."

Adalyn grabbed his hand and tugged him down to their level. "Thank you, thank you. THANK. YOU."

"Shh." He wasn't entirely sure how he should react and ended up going with what felt natural to him. He knelt next to them on the dock, wrapping his arms around them both. "Shh, you're safe. You're both safe."

A sharp whistle snagged his attention, and he glanced toward the path. Zenko Marks held a set of keys up high and pointed to a golf cart. Rory gave him a thumbs up. He understood the offer and was grateful for it. "What do you say we go get a shower, some food, and find somewhere comfy to sleep?"

"Yeah, I'm starving." Sam wiped his nose with his sleeve and Adalyn caught him, produced a tissue from somewhere Rory couldn't see, and wiped it for him. Something she'd probably done a million times and taken for granted before. But Rory knew she never would again. "May I have French toast?"

"Yes, baby, I'll make you French toast."

Rory helped them both to their feet and led them up the path to the golf cart. He offered his hand to Adalyn and winked at her when she accepted and allowed him to help her into the cart. "Sam, you wanna help me steer?"

"Yes. Please."

"Awesome." Rory climbed into the seat behind the wheel and helped Sam climb onto his lap. "Where are we going, Beautiful?" He started the engine.

"Toward the main house." She pointed in the direction the rest of the vehicles had taken. "But we go right at the blue signpost. The second one, not the first one."

"Blue signpost number two." Rory eased his foot down on the power. "Got it. You ready, bud?"

"Yup." Sam had two hands on the wheel and stood between his legs. "Let's rock it." Shakily at first until Sam got the hang of the wheel and Rory got the hang of the pedals, they inched their way up the path.

"Careful, bud." Rory put one hand on the bottom of the steering wheel, helping to guide the golf cart around the turnoff. "We don't want to send your momma out the window."

"Yeah." Sam's tongue stuck out the corner of his mouth in concentration. "Help me keep her safe, please."

He fucking hated that an eight-year-old had to worry about keeping his mother safe. An eight-year-old should be worried about figuring out what he wanted from Santa or which baseball he wanted to toss around this weekend. "Always, bud, I promise." Against his shoulder he could feel Adalyn snickering but didn't understand why. "What's so funny about wanting to keep you from flying out the window?" Her snickers turned to outright laughing. "Is this what hysteria looks like?" He exchanged glances with Sam.

Sam lifted one shoulder. He didn't know what was going on either.

"I'm not—I'm not hysterical or losing my mind." She spoke through fits of laughter. "I'm just remembering how Noble got stuck in the window of the Ape truck and Zenko videoed it."

There was absolutely no reason on the planet for him to be jealous of Noble Bauer or Zenko Marks. Yet here he was with neon green flashing in his head. Neither of those men would ever betray their partners, just as neither would step into his lane. But he wanted the ease with which she laughed about those two idiots for himself. "What's an Ape truck?"

"You know those little three-wheel trucks they have here on base?"

He grinned. He didn't know Red Squadron had those, but he'd been to Italy enough to know exactly what she was talking about. "Tell me you have a copy of that video?"

"I don't have a phone or my computer." She pointed to the path to her little guest house. "Go that way."

"Okay." He and Sam steered the gold cart where she directed.

"But I'll ask Max to send it to me when I get a phone or a computer."

"I'll make sure you get them ASAP."

"This is us." She pointed to her cute cottage with the white shutters and the window boxes full of flowers. It looked straight out of a fairy tale.

"Jeez, Red Squadron are domesticated." He stared at the little house. "I was expecting a CHU or something."

"What's a shoo?"

"CHU." He corrected Sam. "Choo like the sound the train makes. It's a house made out of a shipping container. We lived in them on military bases in the Middle East."

"Okay." Sam nodded. "Will you show me one?"

"Absolutely, bud." He slowed them to a complete stop and set the brakes. "When we get back to Montana, I'll show you one." As soon as he heard Adalyn's inhale, he knew he'd screwed up.

"Yay." Sam bounced out of the cart, landed on his feet, and ran toward the windows to look at the flower boxes and peer into the bird feeder which hung on a metal stake with a couple of swirly hooks.

Rory turned to her. "I'm sorry, I spoke out of turn. I should have talked to you about coming home with us first."

"It's okay. I spoke to Eedana about it yesterday," she reassured him. "Noble and Max made me talk to her to figure out what's safe for me and Sam."

"Eedana railroaded you, huh?"

"Pretty much."

He made a mental note to pick up a souvenir gift for Logan's woman. If he'd had to try and persuade Adalyn it was better to come back to the United States, he'd have fucked it up for sure. He'd been dreading having them go back to their old life of traveling on the road. But now he had more time… he needed to figure out if she wanted to do the same things with that time as he did. He jumped out of the golf cart and jogged around to the other side to lift her out.

Adalyn wrapped her arms around him and squeezed tightly. "Thank you," she whispered softly.

"You're welcome." He soaked in the hug much like flowers

soaked in water after spending the day under a ninety-degree sun.

"Mom?"

"Coming." She pulled back. "Let me get him in the shower and in some clean clothes and then I'll make all three of us some of the French toast sandwiches he asked for before he was…"

"Don't think about it, Beautiful." He pressed a sneaky kiss to the top of her head. "There's time enough for that at an appointment with a shrink. Until then, revel in the fact he's back."

"Mom, I'm starving."

"I know." She pulled away and led Rory up the garden path and opened the door. "The first thing you need to do, Mister," she grabbed Sam and scooped him off his feet, "is shower."

"Mom." He squealed a happy sound which reminded Rory of his nieces and nephews when they were happy.

"Make yourself at home," Adalyn called. "There's a spare bathroom in that door." She pointed to a door next to the kitchen. "Feel free to use it if you like. We'll be out when Sam is squeaky clean."

"Thank you. I might take you up on that if I can locate my sh—gear." He turned at the sound of an approaching vehicle. Spotting Logan coming down the path, he turned back to Adalyn. "Are you sure you want me to stay?"

"Yes."

"Don't leave," Sam cried. "You promised."

"I'll stay as long as it's okay with your mom."

"Bro, are you coming with me or do you want your go bag?" Logan lifted the bag one-handed and waved it at him.

Rory didn't answer Logan but looked to where Adalyn and Sam stood at a bedroom door, watching him. "Are you sure you want me to stay?" he repeated.

"Yes."

"Yes."

They both replied, their heads nodding in unison. He knew his smile was huge when they did the jinx thing, but he didn't even care when Logan gave him a shit eating grin as he tossed the go bag out of the cart and took off.

Rory walked down the path to pick up his stuff and returned to the little house. Shutting the door behind him… closing them into this space was twofold. It was closing them in to keep them safe, but also closing them inside his heart. Now he just had to figure out how to keep them there.

CHAPTER TWENTY-SIX

ADALYN PULLED the door of her tiny bathroom almost closed. At eight, Sam didn't want his mom watching him in the shower. But she needed to check every inch of him to make sure he was okay. "Mom?"

"I'm still here." She leaned her head against the wall next to the door. "I'm just going to open some of the Amazon boxes that have clothes for you in them. But if you call for me, I'll hear you."

"Okay." Sam's voice was partially muffled by the sound of the water. "You won't leave, right?"

"No, I promise."

"Good."

God, how did she deal with this? There was so much to do. He needed to be checked over by a doctor. She needed to organize therapist visits. Find out where Sally and all her stuff was and figure out how she was going to get that all back to the US. There was just so much to do, and she had no idea how she was going to manage it all.

I can do this.

I have to do this.

If I don't, then who will do it?
Fudge freaking crap sticks.

She squeezed her eyes shut and concentrated on breathing. In and out. In and out. Probably just as important as remembering how this breathing thing worked was not allowing the churning in her stomach to win. Her kid didn't need to see her puking her guts up. She'd managed to stay almost sane while they were focusing on getting him back, but now he was here and she knew he was safe, every ounce of strength she had wasn't going to be enough to stop her from melting down. She just had to keep it together long enough for him to be asleep and he couldn't see it. She straightened off the wall at a knock at the bedroom door and crossed the room to open it.

"How is he?" Rory's head was damp, and he'd changed out of the camo clothing he'd been wearing and into jeans and a well-worn band T-shirt, indicating he'd had one of the fastest showers in history.

"He's still in the shower."

"Mmh," Rory murmured. "And you, Beautiful, how are you doing?"

"Surviving." She didn't know how else to describe it, because telling him she was screaming inside where no one could hear would result in questions she didn't have the energy to look for answers to right now.

"Liar." He softened the word and tugged her into a hug. "Lean on me. You've got this, but you don't have to do it alone."

She appreciated that more than he would ever know.

"Let him see you're upset too. That you struggle to deal. Because seeing he's not the only one will teach him it's okay to talk when he's scared or worried."

"Do you moonlight as a therapist?"

"No." Rory rubbed his chin on the top of her head. She

loved that she fit right in there; it was as if this spot in his arms was made just for her. "But when you do the job I do, you learn pretty fast that bottling shit up and lashing out because of it gets you benched faster than that freaky ass doll in the movies' head can spin."

"Mom?"

"I'm in the hall talking to Rory," she called back. "I'll be right there." She pulled out of Rory's arms. "I—um—I gotta go…"

"Go on." He didn't seem to feel one little iota of the awkwardness she was feeling. She knew how to parent alone. She knew how to do everything alone… this having someone to share her troubles with… this she had no idea how to handle. She turned at the door and gave him a small half wave before retreating to the safety of her room where she didn't have to deal with the swirl of emotions which had nothing to do with Sam and the ordeal they had both gone through.

"Sam?"

"I think the towel shrunk!" he yelled from the bathroom. "It doesn't cover my butt."

Welcome back to the real world. Where everyday problems can be solved by your kid picking the wrong towel off the rack.

"Use the blue one. The pink one is a hand towel." She grabbed the stack of Amazon packages and dropped them on the end of the bed. Normally, she'd be all about washing new clothes before wearing them. But there was no freaking way she was putting the clothes Sam had taken off back on him. Those things could just walk themselves right into the trash can.

"Oh."

She found the box of Superman underwear, a pair of basketball shorts, and a clean blue T-shirt, and took them to the bathroom door. "I'm going to stick my hand in with your clothes, okay? Try not to drop them on the wet floor."

"Mom, I'm not a baby."

"I know."

But you're growing up way too fast.

She didn't dare say that out loud though. By the time Sam emerged from the bathroom she had schooled her face into what she hoped was a happy mom face, and not an 'I was so scared I'd lost you' face. "Are you ready for food?"

"Yeah."

"Did the guys not feed you?" She'd have to ask Rory if they'd remembered that eight-year-olds needed feeding multiple times a day.

"Yeah, cardboard spaghetti."

"What?" She ran past him and into the kitchen. "You fed my kid cardboard spaghetti?" She surveyed the kitchen and narrowed her eyes at Rory.

He glanced up from the bowl of eggs he was whisking together. "No, I gave him my MRE." The eggs on the beater dripped onto the floor when he moved his hand too much. "I swear it was just a meal ready to eat and not cardboard."

"Sure tasted like it." Sam pulled out a chair and pushed it across the floor to kneel on it, putting him level with Rory next to the counter. Clearly her son was more than comfortable with him, which was a relief.

"It does," Rory agreed. "But it is real food." He leaned his head down to whisper something in Sam's ear that she couldn't hear, but Sam climbed off his chair and went to grab a second one, scooting it next to his.

"Sit here, Momma. Rory's cooking."

"Thank you." She stopped herself from calling him baby in front of Rory as she figured that wouldn't earn her any brownie points. Especially as it was completely adorable how Sam was mirroring Rory in all he was doing. "You do know how to cook, right?" she asked Rory.

"Yup."

"More than cardboard MREs?"

He snorted and flicked some of the flour Sam had been pouring onto a plate under his watchful eye. "Touché."

She didn't know how it happened, or even who started it, but the next thing she knew she was chasing Sam around the kitchen, flicking flour at him.

"Hey!" she squealed when Rory picked her up from behind.

"I've got her, bud. Quick, dump some of that flour on her head."

"You are meeeeaaaaaaan. Oh my God." It was difficult to form words when she was laughing so hard. She covered her face with her hands as Sam did as Rory instructed and dumped a handful of flour onto her head. She wriggled free and bolted for the other side of the kitchen. "Sam, help me, quick, it's Rory's turn."

Sam and Rory watched her scoop some of the beaten eggs into a mug with their eyes wide. She waved a second cup at Sam. "What are you waiting for? Get him."

"Yay." Sam bounded across the kitchen and took the mug of eggs she offered. "You're going to get it," he warned Rory.

The look in Rory's eyes dragged laughter from somewhere deep down in her belly out of her. "Is the big bad soldier afraid of a little egg?"

"Damn straight." Rory turned and bolted for the door with her and Sam chasing after him. Sam nailed him with his mug of eggs right by the gate. Rory vaulted over it with eggs dripping down his back. She had to wait for Sam to open the gate for her so she could chase after him. She may not be a warrior, but a food fight was totally her jam.

"Get him, Mom. Get him."

She put on a burst of speed at Sam's encouragement and ran faster, almost dropping the eggs all over herself when Rory skidded to a stop and stepped to one side. All she could do was watch in horror as the plastic mug flew out of her hand and landed right in the middle of Dalton's chest.

"Oh, crap."

Rory doubled over next to her.

"Stop laughing, you jerk."

"Yeah, you jerk." Dalton's voice dripped with sarcasm. "Your woman just dumped eggs all over me, stop fucking laughing."

"I can't, the look on your faces." Rory snorted. He placed one hand on Sam's shoulder when her son leaned against him. "You should see your faces."

"Jerk." She couldn't help herself and smacked at him. "You moved out of the way on purpose."

"I was coming over to see if y'all wanted hot dogs or pizza." Dalton swiped at the eggs on his chest and smacked at Rory's T-shirt, spreading the gooey mess.

"Stop that." Rory knocked Dalton's hand away.

"Just sharing the love, brother. Just sharing the love." Dalton winked at Sam. "Whatcha say, kid? Pizza or hot dogs for dinner?"

"Hot dogs please." Sam glanced at her. "Can we, Mom?"

She was never going to be able to look Dalton in the face after covering him in freaking eggs. "Of course, we can."

"Go get cleaned up," Dalton ordered. "We'll start the bonfire as soon as you get to the main house." He turned and strode away.

She dropped her face into her hands. "He's going to hate me forever."

"Nah." Rory grinned at Sam. "But his revenge may be epic."

"Great," she groused. "Okay, back into the showers. We need to get cleaned up again as we are going over there for dinner, and I'm not having them think my family is a trailer park after a hurricane."

"Yes, Ma'am." Rory turned Sam toward the house. "Come on, bud, we can share the big bathroom and your mom can use hers; that way we can eat faster. Deal?"

"Deal."

CHAPTER TWENTY-SEVEN

Investigations are still ongoing into the case of four Americans, two French citizens, and one Russian citizen who were arrested in Montenegro on suspicion of human trafficking earlier this week...

He made sure the TV was low enough that he could barely hear it. He ignored the news anchor and counted the kids being taken out of the house on the footage behind her. Leaving those boys there had ripped at something inside his soul. Sometimes you had to make a shit choice in a shit situation and try to make the best of it. It didn't make it suck any less though. If he had to be the one making the tough calls, he didn't know how he'd deal with it though. Thankfully, that was Trev and Dalton's role.

"Did they save the other boys?"

He lifted his head off the couch and hit the button on the TV to turn it off. Adalyn didn't need to see it. "Yeah. I counted twice to make sure they had everyone."

"What happens now?" She hovered near the end of the couch as if unsure of her welcome. "To the people arrested and the children."

"The authorities in Montenegro will work with the countries those children are from and organize reuniting them with their families." He swung his legs off the couch to make room for her. "The people arrested are going to jail."

"But what about King and Kristin?"

"King has slithered back into his underground hole." He knew Dalton was all kinds of furious about that. "But he'll get his, the noose is tightening. Those people arrested there will lead to other targets. His empire will fall, it's only a matter of time."

She sat next to him and tucked her feet under her. "And Kristin?"

"All our intel guys are working on that." There was no way she needed all the details. Kristin was also a fight for another day. "But there's something hinky about that whole situation with her."

"I agree." She leaned her head on his shoulder. "It makes no sense to me that she'd turn on Eedana. They've been friends for years and years. There has to be a reason or something…" She trailed off.

"Sometimes good people fuck up and do stupid shit." Oh, boy, didn't he know that better than most? "It doesn't make them bad people, especially if they try to fix it."

"Did she? Try to fix it, I mean?"

"I don't know." He wrapped his arm around her. "We might never know. I guess we'll just have to wait and see."

"Damn, I feel like if I put this in a book and left it as an open plot line, people would lose their minds."

"Yeah. But sometimes real life doesn't give you closure. And sometimes people just fuck up and everyone around them has to deal with the fallout." The last two nights he'd enjoyed just relaxing on the couch with her, keeping vigil for Sam's nightmares as they waited for the dawn. "Tomorrow, we go home. Are you ready for that?"

"Yes, I can't wait to see Eedana. Hopefully my stuff out of Sally arrived too. I can't wait to have my own clothes again."

"I know…" Movement out of the corner of his eye drew his attention. "Are you okay, bud?"

"Can I sleep in here with you?" Sam rubbed sleep out of his eyes.

"Sure, you can." Rory moved to get off the couch to make room for Sam to lie on the couch next to his mom. He could sit on the chair across from them.

"Why don't we all go sleep in my room?" Adalyn rose too. "The bed is bigger than the couch and we'll all have more room."

"Are you asking me to sleep with you?" His eyes widened when he realized how that sounded. Thankfully, Sam didn't pick up on the tension which immediately ratcheted up between them.

"Stop it, you." She smacked him lightly on the belly. "Behave." She steered Sam toward the bedroom.

"I'm not sure I want to," he whispered softly in her ear as he followed her and Sam to the bedroom.

"Me either, but stop it," she whispered back.

Yes. Thank fuck. Yes.

After settling into bed with Sam between them, Rory linked his fingers into Adalyn's and sighed a happy sound. "Night, Beautiful."

"I like you call my mom beautiful," Sam whispered sleepily.

"Me too, bud, me too." He could already see Sam's eyes closing and knew it wouldn't be long before he slept again. If he needed both of them to curl around him for the next year so he could sleep, then Rory would do it for him, no questions asked. He might have blue balls from sleeping next to Sam's beautiful mom, but he could deal with that too.

"Night, Rory."

"Night, Beautiful." He closed his eyes and counted silently backward in his head, just as he did to send himself into a combat nap when he needed to. He glanced at the sleeping child between them and lifted her hand, turned it over, and pressed a kiss to her palm. It would have to do for now. Tomorrow night, they'd be back home in Montana. He hoped that meant they would be in his bed, in his home, and working on making it theirs.

"Are you ready to see your new home?" The flight across the Atlantic had gone smoother than normal, but Rory was so ready to get off this tin can with wings and onto the ground. Sure, it was a fancy tin can with all the bells and whistles, but compared to the C-130s they typically used, the private jet just felt a hell of a lot more vulnerable.

"I'm excited." Adalyn almost bounced in her seat. He wasn't sure if it was excitement for herself, for Sam, or all of them. Either way, he'd take it.

The ranch they were circling around was the only adult home he'd known outside of bases where he'd been stationed around the globe. He hoped they liked it here. That this place could become to them what it had to him. A place of refuge, where he was accepted for who he was, quirks, PTSD, and all.

"Me too."

"Here, let me help you with your seat belt." Rory reached across Sam's lap and helped him secure the belt for landing. "It's the middle of the night so you can't see much. But if you look out the window, you'll see the lights of the ranch and the runway."

"He's loving this," Adalyn whispered softly. "Thank you for letting him have the window seat."

"Me too." It was true. Sam was an awesome kid and seeing the world through his eyes was one hell of an experience. "Everyone should sit at the window seat at least once in their lives."

"I agree, but this time is way different than a normal plane." She gestured to the plush surroundings. "I'm almost afraid to touch something in case I break it."

"Right?" He ran one finger along her arm, then turned his hand up. Every single time he'd done this over the last few days, she'd placed her hand in his and it blew his mind every single time. "But if we break something, it can be fixed."

"I never want a bill from having to fix something on this plane. Because I'm sure I'd have a heart attack about five seconds after I opened the envelope."

"Same." He nodded to Sam. "Look at his face."

"I'm making nose art on the window." Sam pulled his face back from the glass. "Do you think it will stay there?"

"I don't know, but I hope you're planning on cleaning it," Adalyn deadpanned. "Nose art is out of the mom leagues."

The plane touched down smoothly and taxied toward where he knew the hangar was located. His truck would be there waiting for them just where he'd parked it when he'd left to go to Morocco on vacation.

"Where do we go now?"

"Home with me." He helped first her and then Sam out of their seats before grabbing their stuff from the lockers. "We'll figure out the rest tomorrow."

"Sounds like a plan."

"Are we there yet?"

"As soon as the door is opened, yes we are." Rory nodded to where the flight attendant Lina had insisted they needed stood waiting at the door for Dalton's orders to open the plane. Like most of Nemesis Inc.'s staff, he knew the man was former military who'd needed a soft place to land after a rough separation from the Army and a divorce which had cost him everything.

"Open her up, Spider," Dalton called. "We're all set."

"Roger that, Sir." Spider turned the handle on the door and pushed it out and to the side, then stepped back to allow them to disembark.

"Thanks, man." Rory nodded to him as he stepped out into the night with Sam right behind him and Adalyn behind her son. Even here at the ranch where he was most comfortable, he took his promise to protect them seriously. If a bullet was going to come out of the dark, it would have to come through him first.

"Bootsy!"

He could feel her hand on his waist as she peered around him and Sam. He barely had time to pull Sam to one side to make room for Eedana. From the determined look on her face, he thought there might be a real danger of her running right over him as she aimed directly for Adalyn.

"Dana normally greets me like that." Logan came to a stop next to him. "Tonight I could be chopped liver for all she cares." They watched the two women fall into each other's arms, hugging and talking a mile a minute. "Get ready for tears, boys," Logan advised. "Lots of tears, bring tissues or you guys are gonna need a boat to get to the house instead of your truck."

"If we need a boat, then you're going to need one too, Mr. Logan. Because that's your wife crying all over my mom."

"That's my boy." Rory high-fived Sam, but turned worried eyes on his friend. "Those are happy tears… right?"

"Yeah, brother, those are happy tears." Logan slapped him on the shoulder. "I'm going to see if I can remind my woman that I exist, too, and was also on the plane tonight." He made a beeline for the women, but paused and called over his shoulder, "You coming?"

CHAPTER TWENTY-EIGHT

Knock. Knock. Knock.

Adalyn jerked upright on the bed. Sleeping in a strange place was always confusing for her, which was why she'd brought Sally for traveling in rather than renting Airbnbs or similar short-term rentals. Those were okay for a night or two, but she much preferred her own bed. It had been almost dawn by the time they'd made it to Rory's apartment in what he called Alpha house.

Knock. Knock. Knock.

"Rory, Sam?"

They'd been here when she'd fallen asleep. She hadn't heard them leave, but surely they wouldn't go without telling her. She threw back the covers and got out of bed. Rory would know she'd freak if Sam disappeared... right?

He's male; they aren't always the sharpest tool in the shed.

Understatement of the year.

She went down the hallway toward the living room, expecting to see the boys there watching cartoons just as they had most mornings in Italy, and frowned at the dark screen over the fireplace.

Knock. Knock. Knock.

"The door, you idiot. There is someone knocking at the door." She took a second to glance out the peephole. Not that she thought anyone could break into the building, considering Rory had used some type of scanner to read his palm print before they'd been able to get in last night. But after the week she'd had there was no way on earth she was taking any chances. "Dana." She threw open the door. "Is everything okay?"

"Yes." Eedana handed her a Yeti Rambler. "Careful, it's hot." She leaned against the wall and gestured to a door close to where they stood. "I live there, and I figured you were about ready for some coffee."

"We're neighbors?" Adalyn sipped cautiously from the mug and sighed happily. "I can't believe we are neighbors."

"I know, right?"

"I can't find Rory and Sam…"

"They've probably gone over to the canteen to grab some food. Did you check for a note?"

"No." Lord, she was an idiot. She turned away from the door and walked back to the bedroom to check the bedside table and the bed but found nothing. "No note." She frowned at her friend when she saw her still standing outside the door. "Why didn't you come in? What are you, a vampire? Get your butt in the house."

"I didn't want to just assume."

"Are you crazy?" Adalyn shook her head at her friend. "It's still a house if it's an apartment… right?"

"I think so." Eedana hugged her back. "I call our place my house."

"Good, because I'm not good with words."

"Says the bestselling author." Eedana grinned at her. "There are a whole bunch of superfans who'd beg to differ."

She pulled out her phone. "Lemme text Logan and see if he knows where Rory and Sam are."

"Thank you." She didn't want to be worried, but she just couldn't help herself. "I'm probably being stupid about it..."

"No, you aren't, Bootsy." Eedana headed for the couch and sat down. "Rory leaving with Sam was a silly thing to do. Especially without telling you. Being male isn't an excuse either." Eedana wagged her finger. "I know what your characters say when this shit happens." Her phone beeped in her hand. "Yeah, they are eating brunch with the guys." She side-eyed her. "Your man is an idiot."

She flopped back on the couch. Other than some stolen kisses and hand holding, there had been nothing to tell her what exactly Rory was to her. "I don't know that he is my man."

"Lies."

"I'm serious." She was going to ignore the heat she could feel marching up her neck. If she ignored it, then it wasn't happening. "I mean we haven't..." She trailed off.

"I cannot believe I am sitting on Saffron R. Cassidy's couch discussing her sex life." Eedana flopped her arm across her face, covering her eyes.

"Stop it." But Eedana's teasing was so freaking welcome, a touch of normality in the messed-up chaos which had become her life. "Everything is happening so fast," she said. "Everything... but that."

"Sex. You can say the word, you know, Bootsy."

"This isn't about sex."

"I know, I'm just teasing you." Eedana sobered. "I think I've been hanging around with Willow and Lina too much. You'll meet them later. They are Dalton and Cormack's wives."

"I know which one Dalton is, but who's Cormack?"

"Jeep." Eedana sipped her coffee. "And we spoke about it before so I know you are changing the subject."

"I'm not trying to, I swear, my brain is just jumping around." She hid her face behind her Yeti. "I don't know what's happening between us," she admitted. "He hasn't left us since he brought Sam back to me. He brought us here."

"You're sleeping in the same bed." Eedana nodded toward the hallway. "At least that's where you went to look for a note."

"With Sam between us." She might as well give her all the details. "He doesn't want to sleep alone, and honestly I'm not even mad about it."

"Is Rory?" Eedana asked. "Mad about having Sam in the bed with you, I mean."

"No. Quite the opposite. At least I think so."

"I think he's being careful," Eedana said slowly. "If a man like that wanted only burn up the sheets sex, he could go to any bar and pick up a woman there, do his thing, and walk away. But you…"

"But me…"

"He brought you home with him, Bootsy." Eedana waved her hand around the room. "And he brought you to his place, *and* didn't put you and Sam in one of the guest suites. That has to mean something…"

"It does."

She dropped the Yeti when Rory spoke, and she whipped around to look at the door. "Oh my God."

"Hi, Beautiful."

She glanced behind him, looking for Sam.

"He's gone to see the horses with Logan, Jeep, and Willow," he explained. "Eedana, they're waiting for you at Bison's stall."

"I can read the room." Eedana got to her feet and leaned

down to whisper in her ear, "Burn up those sheets, sister… because he's got way more than an itch for you."

Oh. My. God.

Jeepers, she'd been repeating that sentence in her head so many times this week that her internal voice was even starting to sound like the annoying woman from *Friends*.

Rory stepped into the room and pinned her with a stare. He kept his eyes trained on her as he spoke to Eedana. "Shut the door behind you, Eedana."

"Of course." Eedana, the witch, leered at her and fanned her face behind Rory's back. "Have fun, you two."

She watched him warily as he stalked across the room toward her. "I…"

"If you don't want this, want me, tell me now."

Oh my, his voice is all growly.

"Adalyn."

Whoops, she wasn't supposed to be devouring him with her eyes. He'd asked her a question.

"Beautiful, I need you to tell me yes or no."

The uncertainty creeping along the edge of his voice snapped her focus back to his face. "Yes, I want this. Us."

"Thank fuck." He swooped down to plant a hot hard kiss on her lips.

She opened for him, and his tongue swept into her mouth as he braced his arms on the back of the couch on either side of her head. That moan couldn't possibly have come from her. But she knew it had. He licked, tasted, claimed, and invaded her mouth until neither of them could breathe, and he released her.

Her breath sawed in and out of her lungs. She would remember how to breathe in a second as there was no way she was missing this by passing out from lack of oxygen. "Rory, God."

"I'm no god, Beautiful, just a man." He picked her up, took

her spot on the couch, and settled her on his lap. "Your man, if you'll have me."

"There's Sam…"

What are you doing?

Are you insane?

Are you trying to get him to stop?

"Yes, there is Sam." Rory nodded solemnly. "And I swear to you he comes first always. We'll just have to get creative on finding some time for us. But never at his expense."

She hadn't known that was exactly what she needed to hear. The *right* words. In the *right* moment. From the *right* man. This time it was her mouth which claimed his. Between kisses she also managed to find the right words. "Then yes, I want this, us, you."

"There is no going back," he warned her. "This is the start of us. I keep, protect, and…" He paused to make sure she was paying attention. "*Love* what's mine. From this day to our last you'll be mine and I'll be yours."

"I love the sound of that."

"Good."

It wasn't an I love you, but it was so damn close she'd take it. "Is this a relationship?" The last time she'd tried one of those, she'd been young, stupid, and ended up divorced.

"You can call it whatever you want as long as I get to call you mine," Rory said. "You and Sam both." His hands swept up and down her back, sending shivers down her spine.

"Mmh." She leaned into him, slipping her hands under his shirt. He brushed the hair back from her face. "Tell me you are sure," he demanded. "I don't want to…"

"I'm not afraid of you and you won't hurt me." Somehow, she knew that was where he was going with this. "It's been a long time for me. Since before Sam, and I'm out of practice…"

"Fuck."

She thought she had pissed him off when he swore, but when he stood with her in his arms and turned toward the bedroom, she wrapped her legs around his waist and her arms around his neck. A moan slid from between her parted lips when he massaged her ass cheeks as he walked.

He stripped off the T-shirt she wore as he placed her down on the bed. "Jesus, I knew you'd be beautiful, but I wasn't prepared for this lusciousness. My dick is leaking in my pants."

Her hands came up to cover her sleep bra covered breasts. Why couldn't she have been wearing a pretty bra instead of plain black cotton? Rory gripped both her wrists easily in one hand. With the other, he flicked open the bra at the front and peeled back the cups.

"Fucking beautiful." He leaned over her, kissing her deep, his fingers cupping and squeezing her breasts. "I love hearing you whimper and moan," he praised her. "It feeds my hunger for more when I do this." His mouth closed over one nipple and he sucked deep and hard before giving her other the same attention.

"Rory. Oh. Ro—" She panted his name over and over, almost in a chant because her brain couldn't come up with anything else.

"I love hearing my name coming out of your mouth." He captured each nipple between his thumb and forefinger, rolling and tugging, sending sparks of pleasure through her. "I'll never be able to let you go after this."

"You don't have to." She cupped his face with her hand and he sucked her thumb into his mouth, nipping and licking along it.

"Promise me you mean that, Beautiful," he whispered in her ear, nipping at the soft flesh and licking his way down her neck, sucking up a mark on the spot where her neck joined her shoulder. "There." He sounded ridiculously pleased with himself.

"Did you just give me a hickey?"

"Damn straight, Beautiful." He leered down at her. "I want everyone to know you are mine." He claimed her mouth in an almost brutal kiss which set every inch of her on fire. Her tongue dueled and fought for dominance with his. She couldn't let him have everything his own way now, could she? She dug her nails into his sides, grateful they'd finally grown past the quick because if she'd had to miss the growl of pleasure which rumbled from his chest, it would have been an epic tragedy.

He freed her mouth and she sighed his name as her hips bucked up against him in invitation.

"I can smell your pussy from here," he growled. "Lemme see if your panties are wet." He peeled off her yoga pants and ran one finger along her panty line, pushing the material aside. "They are wet, and your pussy lips are beautiful."

If he was going to keep talking like this, she'd just be a human ball of blushing by the time they were done. She could write sex all day if she had to, but it was a whole different ball game to have his running commentary on everything he was doing to her. "If I sink two fingers inside you, will I find you dripping, Beautiful?" he asked.

She closed her eyes and sucked in a shaky breath. "I—um —yes."

"Hmm, you don't sound too sure of that." The sound of her panties ripping was loud in the room only filled with the sounds of their breathing and his voice. He pulled the scraps of material away from her and pushed two fingers in deep, just as he'd warned. "Fuck, you are so tight my dick will hurt you if I don't play a little first."

His words dragged a gasp from her. Through lowered

lashes she could see his jaw clenching as he worked his fingers deeper into her, preparing her for him.

"Say you'll marry me," he demanded as he thrust his fingers deeper inside her.

She clenched her thighs together, arching against him as he curled his fingers inside her. He wanted an answer to that right now. Was he insane? There was no way on this earth she could think of anything but what he was doing to her. She turned her head from side to side, pressing her lips together to stop herself from promising him whatever he wanted to ensure he didn't stop the delicious magic his fingers were doing.

He growled in response, began fucking her with his fingers, and pinched first her right nipple and then her left. "Say it, damn it. I need to hear it. You belong to me. I'm not letting you go."

"Mmh, more please."

"More of my fingers fucking you?" The rat bastard stopped moving. She clenched hard around his digits, silently begging for what she needed. "Words, Beautiful, tell me."

"More please."

"Nope, not those words."

"Rory—please—I need you."

"Good enough. Anyone or anything who tries to take you away from me will be destroyed without mercy."

He leaned over her and pressed a fast kiss to her lips before capturing a nipple between his teeth. He sucked hard before releasing her to sit back on his heels. He ran his thumb over her clit, sending her soaring. "Fuck me, you're beautiful like this."

"Rory, oh, God."

"Beautiful, fucking beautiful." He stroked her clit, pulled his fingers out of her pussy, and used the heel of his hand to rub and stroke and send her soaring into orgasm.

"Rory." She exploded, screaming his name and closing her eyes against the overwhelming ecstasy.

While she was still shakily watching him through lowered eyelids, he got to his feet and pulled off his pants and boxers. Oh, God, she hadn't recovered yet. She shook her head as he placed himself back between her thighs.

"Tell me you want me," he demanded and ran his dick along her wet pussy lips. "Tell me you want to know what it feels like to not be able to figure out where you end and I start."

"Please." The only word she could say came out of her in a pant. Her chest rose and fell as she struggled to take in air. "Please." She moaned and pressed a hand to his chest, running her fingers along the ridges of his muscles which flexed under her touch.

"Fuck, I want more of your touch," he growled. "I want your hands all over me." He grasped her wrist and encouraged her to run her hand down his chest to his stomach. "Please don't stop—"

Her tongue poked out to swipe across her bottom lip. How he shook under her hands drove her onward. She used both of her hands to pet and stroke him, learning every inch of his body they touched. "Mmh."

"You're killing me." Rory dipped the head of his dick between her soaking wet lips. "I wish you could see how fucking beautiful your pussy lips are wrapped around the head of my cock."

She lifted her head from the pillow, trying to see, kissed him, then squeezed her eyes shut against the sensations his dick running over her opening caused. She lay back into the pillows, her hands bunching into the covers. She needed something to hold onto, because she already knew what was coming next was going to be a lot.

"Ready, baby?"

She nodded and he thrust deep. Her cry filled the room.

"Jesus, don't move." Rory squeezed the fingers of one hand into his eyes. "I'm fighting not to come right this second."

Talk about a huge boost for a girl's ego. She wrote about this stuff, where the hero wanted to come the second he was inside his love, but she'd never experienced something quite like this before. She hadn't believed it was possible… until right now.

"You're so wet, and I'm as deep as I can go into the sweetest pussy I've had in my life." Rory stroked his hands down her thighs, and she clenched around him. "I…fuck."

"Please move, please."

"I love how you beg me for more."

He thought that was begging. He'd learn eventually, begging went both ways. She clenched around him again, moving her hips a little as she did so.

"Ahh."

Wow, I love that sound.

She repeated the clench and movement, just to test the groan wasn't a fluke.

"Ahh, shit, baby." His fingers opened and closed into fists. "Please tell me you are ready. If I don't move, I'm going to come just from your clenching around me."

Adalyn clenched again. This time she lifted her hips, pushing against him. A long low moan escaped her mouth as he finally took the hint and begin fucking her slowly.

"I want to fuck you so hard, but I'll hurt you."

The hunger for him to do just that slammed into her, and she met him stroke for stroke. She urged him to move faster, deeper, harder. Her hands clung to his arms as she fucked him back, her pussy tightening and working his dick, needing more, craving more.

"Tell me, Beautiful. Tell me you're mine. Promise you will

belong to me and I belong to you," he demanded before sucking deep on her left nipple.

"I'm yours, Rory. Don't stop, please don't stop. I'm yours. Only yours," she promised.

Rory shifted, lifting one leg higher on his hips, taking her deeper, slower, and with more force as she welcomed him deep inside her.

She sank her fingers into his hair, holding him in place to keep sucking at her breasts. His mouth and teeth should be classified as a lethal weapon; they sent sparks all the way through her body. She wrapped her other leg higher up around his hips, pushing back at him until he finally lost control. "Yesss," she hissed.

Rory slammed into her hard, fast, and as deep as she could take him. As rough and hard as she craved and needed him to.

"Rory." Her orgasm had her crying his name as her pussy milked his dick until it pulsed inside her and he came too.

She hummed a little hum of pleasure as he collapsed on her and she wrapped her arms around him. "Wow."

"Yeah, that works, I think." Rory buried his face in the side of her neck. "Ask me again in a couple of minutes when I recover."

She hummed softly again, her hands stroking up and down his back.

"Careful, Beautiful, that sound goes straight to my balls," he warned. "And if I try that again, I'll have a heart attack." He carefully rolled onto his back, taking her with him. Somehow, he managed to keep them connected while he did it.

"Hmm, you having a heart attack right now would not only be mega embarrassing, but totally and utterly tragic."

"Crap." He froze underneath her. "I didn't wear a condom."

Oh, fuck.

Panic rose inside her, warring with the bliss she'd been feeling.

"Are you on birth control?"

"I—" She shook her head. She wasn't going to lie to him. "No. I never needed it. Getting pregnant with Sam took years…" She caught her bottom lip with her teeth, unsure of how much she needed or should tell him. This conversation while he was still inside her weirded her out.

"I hate that you mention your ex while we are like this." He ran his thumb from her mouth down her neck. "I want to go wipe him off the face of the earth so he's not even a memory." He cupped the back of her head. "I love you. You are mine. It wouldn't me upset if this made a baby."

"It's too soon…"

"Shh." He pressed kisses to her damp cheeks. "If it happens, will you be upset about it?"

She slowly shook her head. With her whacked up hormones and reproductive system, it probably wasn't going to be an issue. But if it did happen… then no, she wouldn't be upset about it. Terrified—that was a whole different story—but upset? "No."

"Good."

"I need to go to the bathroom." She eased off him, wincing as their combined juices ran down the inside of her thighs. "I'll be back in a sec."

"I'll be here." He smiled sleepily up at her. "Don't be too long."

"I won't, I promise." She planted a kiss on the corner of his mouth and fled. She needed a minute to get herself together, and she couldn't do that while he was overwhelming her with his closeness. She should have seen the alpha male inside him. In a way she'd seen and known it. But still, it—he was a lot. A man like Rory would want his own children… right?

She closed the bathroom door behind her and cleaned herself up. She stared at the woman in the mirror, her hair all mussed, and a glow in her eyes. How did she tell him more children probably weren't in her future? God, why did she have to find him now, and why did he have to be just right for her? She blew out a long slow breath, grabbed a bath towel, and wrapped it around herself. She'd tell him. There was no choice. He had to know the complications after having Sam meant she was very unlikely to have more children. "What a way to kill the afterglow," she muttered to herself, took a deep breath, and opened the bathroom door just as the doorbell rang.

Rory swept his gaze up and down her body and climbed out of bed. "That's probably Sam. I'll get it." He rounded the bed and kissed her soundly. "You shower and get dressed, I'll take care of our boy."

She nodded, but he had already turned away to grab a pair of jeans. The doorbell ringing again lit a fire under her butt and for the second time in five minutes she took the refuge the bathroom offered. Maybe by the time she was done with her shower she'd have figured out a way to tell him.

CHAPTER TWENTY-NINE

Two days—two whole days since he'd made love to her, and he'd been careful not to fuck up. He didn't want to overstep, but he needed to know the answer to one important question. "Hey, bud, can I ask you something?"

"Sure." Sam smiled at him over Bison's back. If the kid disappeared for more than five minutes you could guarantee he was here at the stables, loving on the horses.

Crap, now what did he say? How the hell was he having this conversation with an eight-year-old? But he forged ahead anyway. "What would you say if I asked you if I could take your mom out to dinner?"

Start slow. Build up to it.

Hah. Pussy.

"You took us out to dinner yesterday," Sam reminded him. "Do I need to go get washed up again?" The boy's face fell as if showering was the worst torture on the planet.

"No." Rory shifted from one boot to the other. "I mean if I took your mom out—umm—on a date."

"You mean a kissy stuff dinner like she writes about?"

He could feel his eyes widening, and from the snort he

heard from the next stall, whoever was in there was getting a kick out of this. But he couldn't stop now. "What do you know about the kissy stuff dinners?"

"Enough to know if some girl sticks her tongue in my mouth, I'm biting it off." Sam shuddered. "That's a nasty way to choke someone."

He couldn't have stopped the bark of laughter if he'd tried. "Holy shit, bud, come back and say that to me again in a couple of years."

"I don't know if I'll be here in a couple of years." Sam pressed a kiss to Bison's nose. "We always move after a few months."

Rory latched onto the opportunity with both hands. "How would you like to stay here forever?"

Sam squinted at him, his tongue poking out the corner of his mouth as if he was thinking. "You mean kissy dinners and a girl choking you with her tongue means you get to stay at her place forever?"

How the hell was he going to have this conversation when he couldn't keep a straight face? The door of the stall next to them slammed and footsteps hurried away from them. Rory heard the faint sound of dog nails following behind, confirming the foreman had to leave before he choked trying not to laugh at the conversation. Thankfully it hadn't been Logan or he'd never live this down. "Not quite." Maybe he'd better sit down for this. He opened the stall door and sat on a hay bale across from the door. At least from here he could see if anyone else was coming. Being covert wasn't getting him anywhere, so he might as well try asking straight out. "If I wanted to keep you and your mom forever, would you like that?"

"You keep puppies."

"You do."

"We're not puppies."

"You're not." He had no idea where Sam was going with this.

"People take puppies to the pound when they don't want them anymore."

"Not all people are assholes. Some people keep their puppies forever."

"Even the strays?"

"Even the stra—" Fury and rage slammed into him so fast he got to his feet. "Who called you a stray?" He was going to murder the bastard because suddenly it was all making sense. "Who called you a stray, Sam?"

"Umm—" Sam ducked his head behind Bison, using the mini horse for cover.

He'd wait him out if he had to, or he'd ask Adalyn, but he had a feeling her rage may be as big if not worse than his. "Sam?"

"My dad."

Your dad is an idiot.

But he bit back the words. He didn't dare say them in front of Sam. He didn't need or deserve that. "When did he say that?"

"Just before me and my mom bought Sally." Sam's voice was small. "He yelled at Mom to take her stray and leave because he wasn't giving her money no more. She only took me from that house, so I have to be the stray."

On one hand the relief was strong that this wasn't a recent thing, on the other his rage burned bright that poor Sam had those words in his head for so long. "Can you come here and sit next to me, please?"

"Okay." Sam heaved out the word as if the last thing on the planet he wanted to do was come sit next to Rory. But he still emerged from Bison's stall and perched next to him on the hay.

"Sometimes when people are angry, they say things they

don't mean." He better not fuck this up or Adalyn would murder him. "They usually wish they could take the words back… but they can't."

"Yeah."

He nudged Sam gently with his shoulder. "You aren't a stray to me." He figured being straight out was best, and he tried to put it in words Sam could understand. "Neither is your mom."

"You like her, huh?"

"No."

Sam's face fell at his denial. "Oh."

"I don't just like her, Sam, I love her," Rory told him flat out. "I love her, and I love you. See, you can't be a stray. Strays don't have homes. You have one. Mom has one. Well, two homes."

"I don't understand?"

"Your first home is here." Rory placed his hand on his chest. "In my heart, and the second is the house we sleep in." He stopped talking and let Sam think.

"You love me?"

Abso-fucking-lutely!

"Yes."

"You love my mom?"

Is the pope Catholic?

"Yes."

"Oh." Sam's feet kicked against the hay bale. "Does that mean we don't have to leave?"

"I never want you to leave. Ever."

Sam was way too mature for his liking, but he'd figured out over the last few weeks that he was a pretty serious little boy most of the time.

"Okay."

That's it? I'm ripping my heart out here, kid, and you give me okay?

"May I go back to playing with Bison?"

"Sure, don't get kicked, okay?"

"I won't." Sam jumped down from the hay and ran back into the stall. "Hey, RoRo?"

RoRo?

"Yeah, bud?"

"If you're gonna do kissy stuff with my mom, tell her not to choke you with her tongue."

He snorted out a laugh. "You got it, bud." That was permission, right? Confirmation that Sam was okay with him kissing his mom. "You okay with that?"

"Yeah, but I not givin' you mouth-to-mouth when she chokes you."

Rory laughed out loud. It bubbled up from deep inside him, he doubled over, held his belly, and guffawed. "You're killing me, bud, killing me."

"Hey, you two?"

Rory lifted his arm and waved Adalyn over. "How much did you hear?" he whispered softly as she snuggled in next to him.

She handed him one of the two travel mugs she carried. "From where he remembered being called a stray."

He sipped gratefully on the coffee. "It's not your faul—"

"I know." She cut him off. "But this momma bear still wants blood."

He could totally get on board with that. Payment in blood was part of his job after all. "Maybe we can arrange that sometime," he promised her. "Or at least give you a picture of your ex so you can shoot his balls off at the range."

She sipped her coffee and heaved a sigh. "That might be safer than jail time."

He kissed the top of her head, then smooched her on the lips for good measure.

"I can hear you doing the kissy stuff!" Sam yelled. "No choking."

Her eyes widened comically. "What?"

Rory leaned in and whispered in her ear, "He thinks you will choke me if you put your tongue in my mouth."

"Um."

"Yeah, I was kinda lost on how to explain it." He lifted one shoulder. "So I told him to tell me that again in a few years."

She swatted at his arm. "You're kinda good at this stuff, you know that, right?"

"I'm trying."

"Trying matters." She pressed a kiss to his jaw. "Trying matters more than you know."

Lord, he hoped so. He didn't want to fuck this up. He tucked a lock of her hair behind her ear. "How are you doing, Beautiful?"

"What if there are no more?"

"Huh, no more what?"

She glanced at the stall and whispered in his ear, "Babies. What if there are no more babies?"

It would be a goddammed tragedy not to have a baby with her, but it wasn't a deal breaker for him. "Then we love on the child we have and know we are blessed." He watched her carefully out of the corner of his eye. "Is this what's been bothering you?"

"Yeah." She kept her face averted. "After I had Sam, the doctors told me not to plan on more as it's probably not in the cards for me."

"We have Sam," he reassured her. "He's enough, Beautiful, I swear it."

"Men want children of their own…"

He put one finger over her lips. "I may not share Sam's

DNA, and he may not share mine, but what we do share is a hell of a lot more important." He thumbed a tear away from the corner of her eye. "Heart, Beautiful. Sam and I share our love for you, and if I could pick any kid on the planet to be mine, I'd pick him every single time."

"Do you mean it?"

His head jerked up. Shit, he should have known better than to have this conversation here with Sam within hearing distance.

"Baby…"

"Do you mean it?" Sam ignored Adalyn's outstretched hand and demanded answers from him.

"Yes, bud, I mean it."

Sam stared at him for so long Rory was sure he wasn't going to like the response.

"Can we keep him, Mom?" Sam finally looked at Adalyn. "He's our stray and I wanna keep him."

Adalyn's mouth dropped open. She snapped it shut again, then smiled through watery tears. "Yes, baby, we can keep him."

"Yay." Sam jumped on them both. Rory's mug went flying as he caught him. "We get to keep you, just like you get to keep us," Sam told him smugly.

"Yeah, I do."

How the hell had a conversation about wanting to take Adalyn out for dinner turned into this? He didn't know the answers, but as Rory wrapped them both in his arms, he realized he didn't care. They were his, he was theirs. They were a family. His family. Family means love wins.

EPILOGUE

Two months later

"It isn't possible." She clenched her hands together. "Why are you doing this?"

"Because, baby, I have sisters." He dropped the bag on the countertop. At least he'd had the smarts to wait until Sam was in school before he produced the item he'd purchased last week and kept hidden in the glovebox of his truck. "I also know that you haven't had a period once since you've been here." He leered at her. "We've been fucking like rabbits and you know it."

"Shh, mind your mouth."

"Beautiful…"

"You promised it didn't matter."

"Baby." He snagged her wrist and tugged her against his chest. "The only thing that matters is that you are here with me, but if you are, then you need medical car—"

"Oh, for heaven's sake, fine," she snapped. Pulling out of his arms, she grabbed the bag and strode down the hallway. She spun around and pointed one finger at him. "You are never, ever to do this to me again. Ever."

"I promise." If he was wrong, she was never going to

forgive him. Ever. But he didn't think he was. She might not see it, but he did. She was more sensitive, her belly rounded, and the hormones, man, he'd been around enough women and girls to know how the hormones worked.

It wasn't easy being with someone who got weird ass ideas from the voices in her head and jumped out of bed in the middle of the night to write it down before she forgot. But he figured it was balanced by him having to take off on missions at the drop of a hat.

"RORY!"

Her scream startled him so much he froze for a split second before he bolted toward the bathroom. "What happened? Are you oka—" He didn't finish the sentence but swept her into his arms, trying to make sure she was okay as she sobbed into his chest. "Talk to me, Beautiful?"

"It's not—"

Fuck, he'd hurt her by making her take a test because his stupid intuition was on the blink.

"It's not possible. How did this happen?"

"How did what happen, Beautiful?"

"Baby."

"Yes, love?"

She swatted at him with the paper pharmacy bag. "No, you idiot." She smiled up at him. "Your super swimmers did the impossible and we're going to have a baby."

"What? It's not possible, you said…"

"Don't faint on me, you big lug." She snuggled into his chest and kissed his jaw. "I don't know how or why…"

"Doctor, we have to get you to a doctor." Panic slammed into him. This was way different than being the uncle. "We have…"

"Shh." She was reassuring him. "We have time for all that. Right now, I just need you wrapped around me until I believe this is real. Okay?"

"Okay." He scooped her up into his arms and took her to the couch before settling her on his lap. He kissed her long, slow, and deep. "We'll figure this out," he promised. "I love you."

"And I love you."

How the hell had he gotten so lucky? Dalton could have sent any one of his people to Paris. Rory wasn't sure if it was fate or destiny, and he didn't care which. He, Adalyn, Sam, and now this new little one they were to be blessed with belonged together. His little family of three was growing to four. He had truly been blessed.

GET LINA FREE

Dear Reader,
Thank you so much for taking the time to read my boys stories. If you would like to see where Nemesis Inc. Alpha Team began, please sign up to my newsletter and receive a free copy of Lina.

One of my favorite parts of writing is connecting with my readers. From time to time, I send newsletters with the inside scoop on new releases, special offers, chances to win signed paperbacks and other bits of news relating to my books.

Sign up to my newsletter to get your free book:

               Get your free copy of Lina

                      Bella x

FOLLOW ME ON SOCIAL MEDIA:

Facebook: https://www.facebook.com/authorbellastone
Instagram: https://www.instagram.com/bellastoneauthor/
BookBub: https://www.bookbub.com/authors/bella-stone
Amazon: https://www.amazon.com/Bella-Stone/e/B09FBQKBZG
Binge Books: https://bingebooks.com/author/bella-stone
Goodreads: https://www.goodreads.com/author/show/17126278.Bella_Stone

BOOKS BY BELLA STONE

NEMESIS INC: ALPHA TEAM
Dalton
Cormack
Logan
Rory

Nemesis Inc: Bravo Team
Rexar

Manufactured by Amazon.ca
Acheson, AB